Th [illegible] s

Edited by Nicky Winder

Illustrated by Elizabeth Carpenter

Pen Press Publishers Ltd

First published in Great Britain by
Pen Press Publishers Ltd
25 Eastern Place
Brighton
BN2 1GJ

ISBN13: 978-1-905621-97-2

Printed and bound in the UK

A catalogue record of this book is available from the British Library

Cover design by Jacqueline Abromeit
Cover illustration by Elizabeth Carpenter

For more information go to **www.thexmasfiles.com**

To my family,

with love

Yes, yes, there are no penguins at the North Pole. Fine. But someone else will have to break it to them.

About the author

Born in 1965, Nicky Winder unearthed **THE XMAS FILES** as a way of forgetting about her fortieth birthday. She would like to claim that it was excavated as her contribution to English literature, but in fact it represents a twelve-year-long and largely successful bid to avoid doing any form of housework.

Nicky teaches English, and her hobbies include any aspects of gardening that don't involve actually going outside. She also enjoys producing sounds which, in the face of compelling evidence to the contrary, she optimistically describes as singing.

Nicky would like to formally express her gratitude to Martin Noble, even though it means splitting an infinitive in public. Heck, you have to live dangerously sometimes. He has been a stalwart source of editorial advice, faith in *The Xmas Files*, and valiant attempts to protect Father Christmas from several undeserved pen-lashings. Last but not least, Nicky would like to thank her son, whose creative input, inspired suggestions, and culinary tolerance she gratefully acknowledges. This book would not exist without him, or so the letter from his solicitors claims.

Note to publisher:
Please do credit Richard
Moss. He took the photo
and did some much-needed
airbrushing on it.
Thanks!
NW

Contents

Foreword

Dear Reader

It has come to my attention that vicious rumours are circulating to the effect that I do not, in fact, exist. However, you can rest assured that the book you now hold in your hands is concrete (well, paper) proof against such ridiculous notions. Indeed, anyone who claims not to believe in me after reading it will be off my Christmas list faster than you can say 'Yuletide spirit'.

I have also been informed that some people feel my job is not a very demanding one. It is true that I get to play with thousands of state-of-the-art toys, have access to as much free sherry as I can drink, and rake up obscenely large numbers of Frequent Flyer Miles. However, I also have some very weighty responsibilities. Monitoring the viewing choices in the Reindeer TV Lounge springs to mind: Dasher's regrettable smuggling in of a video of *Die Hard 2* recently caused me many a sleepless night.

Another of my duties is answering the letters that arrive on my glitter-frosted doormat at 7.32 every morning. Once I've drafted my replies I pass them over to Tinsel, my secretary, so that she can check them and type them out for me. The problem is, you see, that being a man, I am not very good at typing, whereas Tinsel, being a woman (well, a fairy, actually), functions best when performing simple tasks.

Continued...

~ 2 ~

Tinsel suggested recently that I gather together copies of my replies and publish them. She said it was time people knew the truth about me. I was worried I might get sued by those who'd written to me in confidence, but Tinsel got onto our legal people (a couple of huskies who live down the road) and they said it shouldn't be a problem.

So, on the understanding that any future lawsuits are directed at my secretary and her canine advisors, I'd like to wish you all happy festive reading!

Father Christmas

Tinsel, I hope those huskies know what they are talking about. Don't print this, obviously.

September

My morning coffee, Tinsel? Where is it? And let's start with the letter I sent to that glamorous cookery expert. I don't care what you think, I'm sure she didn't poison me on purpose.

Don't print this.

---

4 September

Dear Nigella Lawson

I am afraid I will have to refuse your kind offer to provide me with seasonal refreshments this Christmas. While I was very grateful for the delicious Home-Made Mistletoe Wine you gave me last year, sadly my digestive system proved to be unequal to the challenge.

Of course, it may not have been the wine that caused my three-week hospitalisation after I'd visited your house. I also had some doubts about the Turkey and Trifle Cheesecake with Crunchy Bauble Topping. And about the Mincepies made entirely from Recycled Christmas Cards.

All in all I feel, Nigella, that I must decline your invitation this year. Mouthwatering as I'm sure your Holly-Leaf Vol-au-Vents are, I don't feel that my stomach is ready for them.

Yours regretfully

Father Christmas

Tinsel, where is that letter I wrote about the appalling job the garage did in fixing the sleigh? I don't want it to find its way into the book; it makes me sound as if I enjoy complaining about things for the sake of it, which is so untrue. Still no coffee, I notice.

7 September

Dear Sir

I have just received my sleigh back from your garage (three minutes and 21 seconds late, I observed with some annoyance).

I demand to know why I have been charged for two sledge-screenwipers when only one was faulty. Also, I notice that you still haven't fixed the flashing fairy light properly – it only works if I nudge the wire with my boot as I'm driving. Not terribly safe when I'm trying to keep my eyes on the roofs and am watching out for pelicans crossing.

All in all I am most dissatisfied with the service provided by your garage, and in future I shall be taking my custom elsewhere.

It's a flyer's market, you know, when it comes to sleigh repairs these days.

Yours in great irritation

Father Christmas

Tinsel, will you get a move on with that coffee? I've waited three days, you know. If I had any clue where the kitchen was I'd be tempted to make it myself.

Also, I can't find the letter from Rudolph's mother. The last time I saw it was when we were experimenting with seasonal origami. You check your paper nativity scene with pop-up stable and revolving donkey; I'll start unfolding my paper robin.

10 September

Dear Mrs Reindeer

I appreciate the concerns you express about the moral standards of Rudolph's companions, but let me assure you that your fears are as groundless as his hooves, ho ho ho.

I accept that the unfortunate publicity Prancer attracted last Christmas may have given you cause for anxiety. However, I'd like to say in his defence that he thought the Rolex was a free sample, and in any case the media blew the whole incident completely out of proportion.

I'm sure it will comfort you to learn that your son will always be under the strict supervision of either myself or one of my assistants, usually an elf or gnome fully trained in first aid and ruminant husbandry.

I have also had a word with Dancer, who now accepts that Rudolph does not at present want to embark on a long-term relationship. It may reassure you to know that I will be harnessing Dancer and Rudolph as far away from each other as possible. She isn't the most reliable of reindeer, and I'm afraid that if there's trouble brewing, she usually has a hoof in it. I've even had to withdraw her flying privileges on a number of occasions after catching her smoking dry lichen behind the sleigh shed.

Continued…

~ 2 ~

Do please rest assured that every effort will be made to guarantee Rudolph's moral well being. I will also insist that he tells me if there's any recurrence of last week's hoof ache.

Yours patiently

Father Christmas

Tinsel, are you growing the beans for that coffee? That drink, on my desk, in one minute! That's an order.

10 September

Dear Samara

Thank you for your letter; sadly some parts of it were obscured by a strange green substance unknown to me, which my secretary identified as 'salad'.

I appreciate your suggestions about 'updating' my 'image', but feel that spraying my beard green might undermine my status as a traditional, fatherly figure. Speaking of which, I accept that my name is slightly old-fashioned, even 'patriarchal', as you point out, but fear that your suggestion for an alternative, 'Parent Christmas', doesn't have quite the same ring to it. I am sorry if you find this response patronising; the last thing I want to do is condescend to sweet young girlies like yourself.

Obligingly yours

Father Christmas

Tinsel, how dare you! I said 'on' my desk, not 'over' my desk. My paperwork ruined, all because of your casual attitude to prepositions. Whatever next?

12 September

Dear Mrs Prytchard-Smythe

Your letter arrived this morning, and I can assure you I will follow your instructions as closely as possible when delivering presents to your delightful little dog. It was especially considerate of you to have Mrs Wuffikins lick the envelope so enthusiastically before you sent it, and I'm told our local dry cleaners, The Washing Well, will be able to restore the corroded swathes of fabric that used to be my favourite cardigan with the minimum of expense.

The jewel-encrusted collar you request may be difficult for me to obtain at such short notice, but the useful statistics you have provided: height, Chinese horoscope sign, favourite Andrew Lloyd-Webber musical, should help enormously. I've got a specialist team of fairies working on the other items of clothing right now. I told them that everything has to match the shade of pink Mrs Wuffikins prefers, and as soon as they stop laughing they'll make a start on the pinning and tacking.

Yours helpfully

Father Christmas

Tinsel, thanks to your witless blunderings, there's now a coffee stain, I notice, on the far right-hand side of my desk. Remove it please.

13 September

Dear Sir

I am writing to query the electricity bill that arrived yesterday, which seems completely excessive. Granted, we do have a large number of fairy lights, but this does not explain the huge amount of electricity for which you are charging us. I showed the invoice to Tinsel, my secretary, and she said that the only way we could have run up such a high bill would be if somebody on my staff had secretly been organising nightly discos, thereby using power for extra heating, lighting and sound.

According to Tinsel, these discos would have to start before midnight and carry on until four o'clock in the morning to account for the sudden increase in energy consumption. I didn't question her in any more detail, as she told me she was really exhausted from lots of late-night dancing, but I leave it to you to reduce your (frankly exorbitant) charges without further delay.

Yours sincerely

Father Christmas

Tinsel, I meant remove the stain, not the whole desk. Now my papers are muddled up and there's Battenberg all over my Knitting Trophy. Bring my desk back now – I'll get rid of the coffee stain myself.

By the way, have you seen my recipe for Fairy Cakes? I feel as if I might be needing it soon.

30 September

Dear Mrs Pallid

I hope that you have recovered from your 'tortuous migraine', 'dreadful cold' and 'agonising sore throat'. I feel I should apologise for the delay in responding, but my secretary inadvertently reversed the sleigh over my left foot after a heated discussion about recipes, so I've been confined to bed for the last fortnight. My only comfort has been occasional visits from Blitzen, one of my reindeer, to cheer my lonely (and once, when he left the window open, snowy) pillow.

Thank you for your letter requesting a First Aid Kit. I agree that it is always good to be prepared; I remember the hideous anguish caused when Rudolph got a splinter in his hoof a few weeks ago. For the whole journey home he described to us in detail the hoof, the whole hoof, and nothing but the hoof. If only we'd had the foresight to pack ear-muffs, a great deal of discomfort could have been avoided.

Please don't feel that you need to write back to thank me for your gift. I would certainly not want to exacerbate your 'excruciatingly painful blister' if, as you fear, your selfish next-door neighbour stubbornly refuses to walk twenty miles to the nearest pillar box to post your reply.

Yours sympathetically

Father Christmas

Tinsel, it just struck me that we need to show how compassionate I am to those in distress. Include the letter to that nice young boy who was so concerned about his sister's choice of presents.

Also, I'm thirsty after all this hard work. Bring me a Sprite.

October

1 October

Dear Anthony

Thank you very much for your charming letter. You sound like a sensible, hard-working lad to me, and I will be sure to bring you all the electronic study aids you ask for, plus the dictionaries and the album for your set of Famous Accountant postcards.

Regarding your sister's Christmas list: I am afraid I cannot prevent her from having an Action Man and a train set, if that is what she has set her heart on. I realise that these items have traditionally been regarded as 'boys' toys', and I do share your fears that your sister is recklessly 'ruining her chances of becoming a happy wife and mother'. However, let us remember that she is only three.

I will close now, Anthony, but I wish you a very happy Christmas. Good luck with memorising all the conversion tables in your Boy Scouts' Diary.

Yours admiringly

Father Christmas

Not that kind of Sprite.

4 October

Dear Neil Quinn

Thank you for the handwritten copy of your novel, *Crisis at Tesco's*. You say you've sent it to every agent and publisher in the country and the most promising response so far has been 'No, this is total rubbish; we're not interested'. That does narrow the field down rather, I agree. So – how to achieve your Christmas wish of publication?

Eventually I gave the manuscript to Tinsel, my secretary, and asked her advice. Since she's female, Tinsel is not a great reader (I believe she tends to enjoy simple children's books, such as *Animal Farm*) but even so she managed to suggest something that sounded vaguely sensible. I must congratulate myself on hitting upon the excellent idea of asking for her input.

Here at the North Pole to think is to act. No sooner was Tinsel's suggestion out of her mouth than we both grabbed some scissors and cut the entire manuscript (not your only copy, I trust?) into tiny fragments, each with one of your unforgettable phrases on it. Then we stuck them inside the Christmas cards we're sending out this year. How better to liven up people's days than with messages like "'Happy Christmas, you crazed old camel,' shouted Jack. 'Can't you see the aubergine's about to explode?'"

As Tinsel said to me on her way to the re-cycling bin a few minutes ago, your writing will 'find its spiritual home at last'. She's got quite a sensitive nature, I suppose, for a mere secretary.

Yours helpfully

Father Christmas

By the way, I've had a request from the Inland Revenue for something they refer to as Tax Returns. I have no idea what they're talking about – any clues?

15 October

Dear Mr Proudfoot

I'm afraid I couldn't read some of your letter as Tinsel, my secretary, carelessly smudged oil over it (she's currently doing a sleigh maintenance course during her lunch hour). I did point out that this was no way to treat my correspondence, but Tinsel just shrugged, wiped her hands on her overalls, and clumped off in what she refers to as her 'DMs'.

Your letter was unusual, as I'm not normally asked to perform tasks for people. However, I see no reason why I can't deliver papers for your newsagents' business while distributing presents. This would indeed be more environmentally friendly than two people following the same route. I hadn't realised before that paperboys on bikes are disastrous to the eco-system, nor that as soon as they become hot from the exertion of cycling there is an immediate increase in global warming. It's refreshing to hear from somebody so concerned about our planet.

Leave the papers out for me and I'll see that they get to the right houses.

Yours, not at all naively

Father Christmas

Tinsel, that note you sent me about Tax Returns looked like total gibberish. It's not clever, you know, using all those airy-fairy long words, even if you do have a First Class Honours degree in Applied Business Management and Corporate Finances. I know you said I can't just bury my head in the snow, but that's precisely what I intend to do.

Has anyone seen my shovel?

30 October

Dear Mr Berry

Thank you for your letter requesting 'a winning lottery ticket'. Sadly this is impossible. If I had access to the winning numbers, do you honestly think I'd have chosen a career like this, with no pension plan, no promotion prospects, and only huge, glitter-coated chunks of job security to recommend it?

I'm sorry if I sound grumpy but I'm not in a very jolly mood this morning. Not only did the post arrive 32 seconds late (I must remember to speak to them about it), but it contained an unpleasant letter from the Inland Revenue demanding to see all my accounts and Tax Returns immediately. *(Note to self: burying head in snow not always best response to tricky situations. Apart from anything else, resultant beard frizziness most unflattering).*

I do hate paperwork, and to make matters worse, my secretary isn't here to help me. The silly creature carelessly slipped over on a remote-controlled toy sleigh I was test-driving in her office. I didn't even realise fairies' wings were breakable. So now she is sitting in the Brownies' Common Room, wrapped in a blanket and drinking brandy, and I'm having to get my own coffee *and* answer the telephone *and* reply to all this morning's letters *and* dig out that stupid paperwork for the Inland Revenue.

Anyway – no, I don't know what the winning numbers are, so I can't give you a winning ticket. All I can suggest is that you adopt the highly scientific method I use myself – assuming, that is, that you have access to an abacus and a blindfolded reindeer.

Continued…

~ 2 ~

Sorry I can't be of more help, but I must go now and write to those Inland Revenue people myself, and then check to see if my secretary can still stand.

Yours apologetically

Father Christmas

31 October

Dear Sir

I received your letter this morning and it has placed me in something of a quandary. You request all sorts of documentation and I don't even understand what some of it is, let alone know how to locate it. Unfortunately my secretary (who usually deals with such matters) is indisposed at the moment following a self-imposed mishap yesterday morning.

In short, I simply haven't a clue about the figures you're interested in. You ask about 'salaries' and 'staff pay-slips', but all I know is that the pixies receive five silver pieces each per week, goblins six, and brownies seven (except for the brownies who work the lift; they only get six). I'm also not sure what 'tax deductible expenses' are; I do run a vehicle 'solely for work purposes', but could I really count reindeer food as a kind of fuel? And does it apply to just the basic reindeer diet, or does it also cover Dancer's fondness for Walnut Whips?

Actually, I think there *were* some documents connected with tax lying around a few weeks ago, but I'm afraid I dropped them in a bucket of glitter-glue by mistake, and although they emerged from it festively sparkly, they were also very sticky, so I decided to throw them away. And we're always knocking over cups of coffee here; if the paperwork doesn't get covered in it initially then it gets used to mop it up with.

I'm sorry, but I really think the only thing we can do is to ignore what's gone on before and start afresh. I'll try to record my expenses, and Tinsel (that's my secretary) and I will try to be more careful with the coffee and the glitter-glue. I think that's the only way forward, really.

Continued…

~2~

Apologies for being vague about all these figures; I really will try to keep track of everything more efficiently in the future. We'll call it quits and start from scratch, eh?

Yours co-operatively

Father Christmas

PS If a present would help to smooth things over, we could certainly oblige. What is your position on Teenage Mutant Hero Turtles, for example?

By the way, Tinsel, after a year's careful deliberation, I've decided to cancel the Annual Reindeer Hallowe'en Party. There was an extremely unpleasant incident last time; I discovered that Prancer had secretly sharpened his antlers in an underhoof attempt to win the Bobbing-for-Apples contest. We can't risk a similar incident happening again; he was a danger to himself and others for weeks afterwards. Break the news to them tactfully, would you? I don't want any unpleasant scenes.

November

1 November

Dear Mr O'Neill

Re: Tax Returns

I received your letter yesterday, but was unable to answer it sooner as I've been trying to wash pumpkin pulp out of my hair and beard following an unpleasant scene. The reindeer responsible has been grounded, naturally, and given a most severe telling off. There were muffled splutterings, doubtless of guilt, as I spoke to him; he was so deeply moved by my twenty-minute speech that he was forced to hang his antlers in shame.

Regarding your letter, I wasn't sure what 'unacceptable response to previous correspondence' and 'full Inland Revenue investigation will be instigated forthwith' actually meant. However, Tinsel, my secretary (who's now fully recovered, you'll be delighted to hear), told me that a lot of people will be visiting the office, and they'd like a guided tour of the filing cabinets, my desk, and the records from Vixen's 'Adopt an Under-Privileged Reindeer' scheme together with the log book for her newly-acquired Lamborghini. So that sounds pretty painless. Mind you, I'm not sure where they're going to stay, because the Happy Sleigh Bell is full at the moment, and the Polar Star Lodge does take paying guests, but only if they have antlers.

Continued…

~ 2 ~

I'll be relieved to have a change of company, actually; Tinsel has been extremely cranky lately. She keeps muttering things about 'fifteen-hour day', 'outrageous working conditions' and 'International Union of Fairies'. I think she's becoming stressed. I said to her 'Tinsel, I realise that preparing for the delivery of millions of presents across the globe is what you might call a logistical challenge, but you've got to be positive. After all, I manage to be calm and unflappable, and to fit in afternoon naps and games of ice golf with Blitzen, so I'm sure you can too'. I think that mollified her a bit; her face went a peaceful shade of mauve and her wand started making cheerful sizzling noises and throwing out pretty gold sparks.

Anyway, I'd be delighted to receive visitors here at any time in the distant future; it's not as if we need plenty of notice to give us the chance to prepare an elaborate cover-up.

Yours sincerely

Father Christmas

Finally, Tinsel! That's got rid of them. I've shown that I have nothing to hide. If they turn up after receiving a letter like that, I'd eat my hat.

4 November

Dear Mr Cope

Thank you for your letter; I'm afraid I'm up to my beard in inspectors from the Inland Revenue at the moment, hence the delay in replying. They even made the reindeer empty their lockers, and asked the dwarfs some pretty searching questions about their E-bay sales of 'Genuine Icicles from Santa's Grotto'.

If Tinsel, my secretary, hadn't started issuing everyone with large gin and tonics, I think we'd feel pressurised, but in fact the atmosphere's becoming quite jolly. And the liquid is for medicinal purposes, for me at least; I'm still suffering from indigestion after the unusual pie I had for lunch today. I'm not sure what the filling was, but I keep finding pieces of furry material wedged between my teeth.

It's slightly difficult for me to concentrate on writing this, as everyone around me is currently singing *Jingle Bells* at the top of their voices. These tax inspectors are very musical. Hang on, I'll just get my glass refilled. That's better! Now then, where was I? There's not much tonic water in this one; it's actually quite strong. *Jingle Bells* has just stopped, which makes it easier for me to concentrate… Ah, but now some penguins have arrived and they've started everyone off on *Flocking Around the Christmas Tree*. Oh well, I'll carry on anyway.

Continued…

~ 2 ~

I liked your letter a lot (yes, Tinsel, I'll have a slice of lemon please); you're obviously keen on recycling because you say you'd prefer your presents to be second-hand. Pick up any old junk I see on my travels: paintings, jewellery, coins and so on, and send it along to you; is that right? No problem at all, Mr Cope, I'm sure people will be glad to have the space cleared in their attics, wallets, safes etc, and the fact that it will benefit your worthy little shop, 'Cope with Antiques', will just be an added bonus.

I have to go now. The Inspection Team Leader appears to be squabbling with an angry pixie over possession of the New, All-Sparkly 'My Little Reindeer' prototype, and things could soon turn very ugly.

Yours sincerely

[*Tinsel, remind me, who am I, again?*]

Father 'Ineptitude' Christmas

Tinsel, I know I was meant to deal with that parking fine a while back, but I stood my potted mistletoe on it, and now it's growing several species of mould. Could you scrape it so that it's clean enough for me to read? I'd do it myself, but unfortunately I don't want to.

4 November

Dear Sir

I am writing to protest at being issued with a parking ticket recently (eleven months ago, to be exact, but I do sometimes get slightly behind with my paperwork), and being instructed to pay a (frankly exorbitant) fine. The ticket was attached to an antler belonging to one of my reindeer (Prancer, actually, and he's still extremely indignant about it. He is currently consulting the Ruminants' Advice Bureau, and may well sue you for compensation in the near future).

In addition to this outrage, my sleigh had been clamped, and a notice left on my sack of presents stating that the clamp would not be removed until February. If it were not for the fact that I happened to be carrying an All-Purpose Clamp Remover designed by my secretary, we would be stranded up there even now, a possibility too appalling to contemplate.

This impertinence occurred even though I had parked my sleigh on the roof in question for less than five minutes, not realising that doing so was prohibited. If double yellow lines had been painted on it, as the ticket claimed, it was certainly too dark for me to see them.

What's more, the traffic warden in question was also the homeowner to whom I was delivering presents, and I would expect him to show a bit more gratitude.

Continued...

~ 2 ~

He should have better ways of spending his time than prowling about on rooftops at midnight, waiting to stick parking tickets on other people's reindeer.

Yours in great indignation

Father Christmas

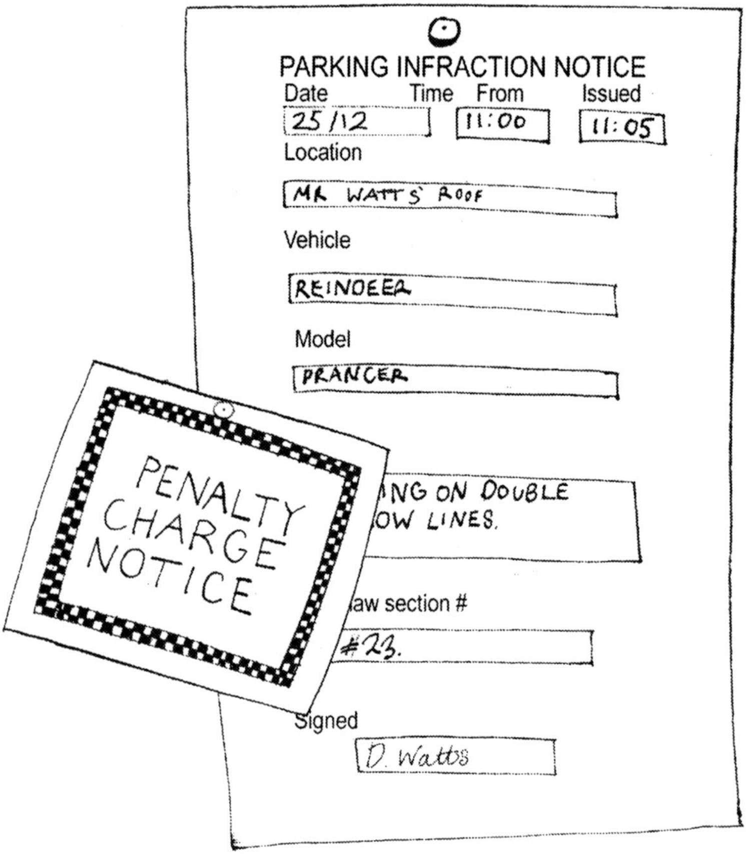

5 November

Dear Mr Cowell

I am writing to express my surprise that I did not get beyond the first round of auditions in your talent contest. Not only was I the sole competitor to be draped in fairy lights and accompanied by tap-dancing goblins, but mine was the only beard to be described as 'fabulous' by one of your fellow judges. You may be reasonably popular in certain circles, but if I don't have the X-Mas Factor, who does?

Yours in deep disappointment

Father Christmas

I hope you're showing people how hard I work, Tinsel. Much of the time I'm completely snowed under. And it's not just about physical demands, either. Perhaps the public needs an insight into the stance I have had to take on moral issues? I'm afraid you'll need to take care of it as I'll be arranging the viewing deck in readiness for the Northern Lights Display this evening. So much cheaper than fireworks, and with the money I save I'll be able to treat myself to that yellow cardigan I spotted in Blitzen's Ruminant at BHS Catalogue.

8 November

Dear Jack

Thank you for your letter. Unfortunately, though, I fear that I will be unable to grant your request. I have no objections, generally, to giving axes as presents – a number of legitimate jobs around the garden* require them. However, I cannot possibly provide you with an axe for your stated purpose, that of 'chopping down a beanstalk'.

Beanstalks have a right to life like every other living creature; they also have the right to a safe environment, and I find it extremely disturbing that somebody of your tender years should be consumed by these violent, destructive tendencies. 'But it's only a beanstalk!' I hear you cry … Only a beanstalk to you, perhaps – but what about the wife and shoots he'd leave behind?

Besides, you said yourself that the stalk in question grew from magic beans – have you checked with the Royal Horticultural Society to ensure that they have sufficient numbers of these beans in stock; that you are not jeopardising the survival of an endangered species?

I will certainly not be bringing you an axe this Christmas, and I hope your beanstalk flourishes; I hope it grows up to a giant.

Yours in complete moral outrage

Father Christmas

* such as chopping up elderly Christmas trees for firewood

Yes, Tinsel, that should do the trick. People are finally getting an insight into the heart that beats beneath the scarlet jacket. What other letters show me in my true colours?

20 November

Dear Mr Beanstalk

Your letter arrived a week ago, but unfortunately I assumed it was an advert for our local garden centre and dumped it in our newly-installed recycling bin (my secretary's idea), from which she has only just retrieved it. Hence the delay in answering.

Having read your letter, I have to say I find your proposals somewhat alarming. It is kind of you to thank me so profusely for refusing to supply your 'enemy' with 'weaponry', as you put it. However, I'm not sure about your plan to flee the area and move to the North Pole before he obtains an axe elsewhere. I realise that you will be in danger if you stay in your own part of the world, but that in itself is one of the problems: the fact that you and your family are victims. If you were white instead of green, had limitless wealth and a huge private income, we'd be only too delighted to offer you assistance. Sorry I can't be of more use, but as you can see, my hands are tied.

Yours sincerely

Father Christmas

PS Have just spoken to Tinsel, my secretary, and apparently I can help you after all. If I don't, it transpires that the entire staff will stage a permanent walk-out, plus Tinsel has said she'll take the law into her wings and set fire to all my knitting patterns. There's only so much emotional pressure a man can take. Welcome to the North Pole.

Not sure I came out of that one looking too good, Tinsel. What else can we do to show the world how concerned I am for the plight of the underdwarf? You'd better get searching; I've got to go shout at some pixies.

25 November

Dear Mr Beefbucks

I have to say I find the suggestions outlined in your letter, which I had the misfortune to receive this morning, totally outrageous. Indeed, I almost choked on my bowl of Frosties. Your plans to open a fast food chain outlet here at the North Pole are completely preposterous, and your proposed takeaway, 'Unlucky Fried Reindeer', will be built here over my dead body.

Furthermore, I will not supply you with reindeer meat under any circumstances, as I consider that keeping animals in captivity for such unsavoury purposes is degrading and inhumane. This is my final word to you on the subject.

Yours, almost speechless with indignation

Father Christmas

Much better, Tinsel. Now people are really starting to glimpse the real me. Keep up the good work while I go and sort out those unreasonable penguins. They've had the nerve to request a Christmas day bonus. Ridiculous – I'm not made of kippers.

December

3 December

Dear Mr Jones

Thank you for your enquiry regarding the renewal of our Christmas order. We will indeed need the same number of turkeys as usual this year. Although six gnomes have joined us in the last few weeks on Work Experience, Tinsel, my secretary, has taken it into her head to turn vegetarian recently, and Sparkles and some of her other more dim-witted friends have copied her. So, forty birds should, as before, see us safely through Christmas lunch, into turkey shortbread on Boxing Day and turkey-flavoured yule log in the New Year.

Thank you too for your Christmas card. I am really busy at this time of year as there is so much for me to delegate, but I'll be forwarding your Christmas card in a couple of days. We're trying to move away from commercially produced cards towards a more personal approach. Although our initial attempts resulted in an unseemly legal battle with an aspiring author, we have decided to persevere, and the card you receive will have been specially designed and produced by a member of our own staff. (Tinsel, I believe, volunteered to do yours.)

Anyway, have a good Christmas, and may I take this opportunity to thank you for providing such a reliable service? I very much look forward to slicing into that delicious meat, containing all those health-giving antibiotics, in the very near future.

Yours sincerely

Father Christmas

18 December

Dear Mr Jones

I was shocked to receive your letter and its highly gruesome enclosure. I can only apologise and beg your forgiveness. What could Tinsel have been thinking of? It's true that I gave the staff producing Christmas cards freedom to create their own designs (although I did make seasonal stencils: stars, angels, chestnut stuffing, and so on, available). I had no idea, though, that Tinsel would allow her silly belief in vegetarianism to unbalance her so much. The picture she drew of that blood-covered ghostly turkey sitting between you and your wife (a good likeness of you both, admittedly) as you tucked into your Christmas dinner, was totally unacceptable, and the message inside, 'Never share thy gory flocks with me', was downright ungrateful. We at the North Pole want you to share your gory flocks with us, otherwise we wouldn't have renewed the order; I don't know what Tinsel was thinking of.

I assure you that this outrage will be dealt with most severely; there is no need at all for you to cancel our order. To do so would be a sad ending to a long-standing business relationship, a relationship that has grown and flourished over the years and has matured into a thing of mellowness and dignified calm. Also, where would we get another forty turkey carcasses at such short notice? May I beg you to reconsider?

Yours, in a painful dilemma

Father Christmas

Tinsel – my mother has just sent me the front page of yesterday's copy of The Northern Plights.

This is beyond belief! I've attached it to this memo so you can see exactly what I'm talking about. I think you'll recognise the imbecile fairy brandishing the 'Justice for Turkeys' placard. My public image is in ruins – just before Christmas, too, when the tabloids will have a field day. Report to my office immediately.

* * *

Minutes of Meeting between Father Christmas and Tinsel

Present: FC, Tinsel
Items on agenda:

1. Disturbing correspondence received from Mr Jones.
2. Consequent lack of turkey ordered for Staff Christmas Lunch.
3. Anticipated rage of staff: gnomes, elves, fairies etc. when acquainted with probable cancellation of lunch.

- FC asked Tinsel why she had behaved so outrageously towards Mr Jones. Tinsel replied that her behaviour had not been outrageous: it had been 'an appropriate and realistic response to politically incorrect tyranny resulting in unmitigated cruelty towards another species'.
- Pause while FC looked up the meaning of 'unmitigated'.
- FC responded that these ideas were all very well, but that Mr Jones was a nice man and did not deserve to receive unpleasant Christmas cards through the post.
- Tinsel identified the problems in applying objective, measurable values to subjective terms such as 'nice' and 'unpleasant'.
- FC said he was developing a headache.
- Tinsel stated that she used the sending of the Christmas card as a vehicle for her personal comment on the unacceptably cramped conditions in which Mr Jones's turkeys were kept, their monotonous diet, and their injection with growth-promoting hormones in excess of EEC regulations. Tinsel

added that anyone who attempted to prevent her from expressing her views fully and directly to Mr Jones would be denying her the basic right of freedom of speech.

- Pause for FC to take two aspirin.
- FC replied that Tinsel definitely had a point (although he was unable to clarify what it was), but what on earth could be done about the Staff Christmas Lunch? Dwarves deprived of their cranberry jelly could turn particularly ugly.
- Tinsel replied that she had matters well in hand, and had already made contact with a local catering firm, 'Yule Tea Without Cruelty', who had agreed to supply all of the Christmas meals during the holiday period.
- FC reported that his head was feeling better.
- Tinsel stated that she did not trust herself to comment, but suggested opening a bottle of vintage acorn juice to celebrate the victory of reason over exploitation.
- FC found corkscrew.
- Tinsel made a toast to the immediate closure of Mr Jones's farm.
- FC raised glass and drank to toast.
- Both parties agreed that the meeting had reached a satisfactory conclusion.
- Meeting closed at 4.30 pm.

Xmas Eve

24 December

Dear Mother

Thank you for your letter, which arrived this morning. Also for your postcard, which arrived yesterday, and your notelet, which arrived the day before that. Thanks also for your recent phone-calls; the 17 so far this morning, 32 yesterday, and those on previous days too numerous to count. The frequency of your phone calls has meant that this is the first opportunity I've had to reply to your letter, postcard and notelet, although I am pleased to say I caught the (penguin) post earlier, and your Christmas card (which didn't involve such a lengthy response) is already on its way.

Your letter did puzzle me somewhat, as I thought we had established the day before yesterday (phone call number 34) that I was definitely going to be home with you on Christmas Day, but that I was unable to be specific (phone call 42) about the precise time.

I realise that my not being able to predict the exact moment of my arrival home is going to put the successful cooking and serving of the Christmas dinner into serious jeopardy; the items you mention specifically being the sprouts (45), gravy (46) and roast potatoes (47). However, please try to understand that I cannot give you any further information at this stage.

Continued…

~ 2 ~

With regard to the rest of your letter: yes, I will remember to wear a knitted vest as well as my scarf, and to take a flask of honey and lemon to drink if I start feeling that I might be developing a cold.

I'm afraid I have to close now, Mother, as the phone is ringing, but I will be sure to write again when I have more news. Luckily tonight's delivery is ready to go ahead, thanks to my excellent organisational skills, so apart from me (and my team of reindeer), the rest of the staff will be able to put their feet/wings/flippers up while I do the hard work.

I remain, as always

Your affectionate son

xxxxxx

[This has been deleted as it is a pet name, personal to Father Christmas, and he does not wish knowledge of it to be extended outside his immediate family – Ed.]

Christmas Eve, Tinsel, and everything seems to be on track for a successful delivery. I know you're heading off for the Pixies' Grand Yuletide Dance in a few minutes, but there are a couple of loose ends I need you to tie up first. I obligingly made a list of them to help you:

Tinsel's Christmas Eve 'To-Do' List

- *Wrap remaining 200,000 presents and put in post with handwritten letters of apology for late delivery*
- *Check all empty warehouses; sweep floors, dust, and polish skirting boards*
- *Carry out audit of current remaining stock levels – all gift categories, please – and work out the projected requirements for the New Year. Remember to bear in mind inflation rates, stock market trends and threatened overtime ban by fairy lights*
- *Ensure that all staff receive their Christmas bonuses; I didn't quite get the chance to count these out but apparently it's very simple. According to my new* How to Calculate Salaries for Mythical Beings Manual, *gnomes get $3x=7y$, pixies get $4h=(x-y)^3$, elves receive $2x^2+3y/4$ and the rest I suggest you make up as you go along*
- *Scrub out reindeer cubicles, ensuring all is spotless in time for the reindeer to put their hooves up on Christmas Day. The poor things will be exhausted by then, and they've certainly earned a good break.*

As soon as you've finished all of this, naturally, you're free to put your fanciest outfit on and flutter the night away. Yes indeed, Tinsel, you SHALL go to the ball.

Xmas Day

Morning, Tinsel. I'm very sorry you didn't manage to get away last night – I was sure those jobs would only take you a few minutes. Perhaps you needed to work a bit harder and faster? Anyway, I'm heading off now to have lunch at Mother's. Can't wait to show her the mobile Blitzen bought me. I've set Santa Claus is Coming to Town *as the ring tone but I enjoy listening to the tune so much I'm reluctant to answer the phone. Of course, I was also delighted with the book you gave me*: An Idiot's Guide to Basic Personnel Management. *I particularly liked the fact that it's so heavy – it will come in handy when I need something to throw at the union rep's head during difficult staff meetings.*

I hope the Christmas Lunch goes well. So glad I can leave all the arrangements in your capable wings.

Have a happy – albeit pleasantly busy – Christmas.

Boxing Day

Tinny, I seem to have mislaid my mobile. I can't see it anywhere, which is very strange, as for some reason (totally unconnected with my recent consumption of 17 bottles of Babycham), I seem to be seeing two of everything else.

New Year's Eve

31 December

Dear Annabel and Sita

I am writing to you both on behalf of my staff to thank you very much for the excellent food and service provided by your firm 'Yule Tea Without Cruelty'. Sadly I missed the Christmas lunch myself, but the staff here enjoyed it tremendously, and have asked me to book your services again for next year. It was also good of you to share some of your recipes with the staff canteen. Most of the items on our menus are now organic and vegetarian, thanks to you, and very popular they are.

Some people might think it 'extremist' or 'unconventional' of me to proceed along these 'unorthodox' lines, but that's just me, I suppose: open-minded. As my secretary remarked the other day, there's enough space between my ears to host the next Winter Olympics.

Yours, about to sample a courgette and cashew nut yoghurt

Father Christmas

Tinsel, I've made a New Year's Resolution. I want to cultivate my mind and let people see how intelligent I am. Make sure that the next few letters show me at my insightful best.

By the way, I'm a little apprehensive about the behaviour of the staff at tonight's New Year's Party, especially given last year's regrettable incidents. I'll be on standby with my mobile switched on (if I can find it), and I'll text you if anyone shows signs of enjoying one too many glasses of Northern Comfort. I'm sure that between us we can ensure that all goes smoothly. Anyone whose conduct is less than exemplary will be punished most severely.

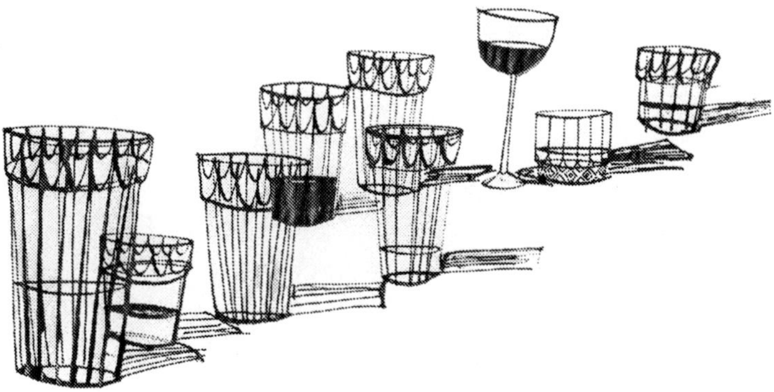

New Year's Day

Tinsel – what can I say?

First person to send me a set of Super de Luxe Wing Upgrades in fluorescent pink gets a video of FC wearing a platinum blonde wig and performing Dancing Queen at last night's office party – Tinsel

Tinsel! Have you been at the fairy liquid again? It's bad enough that Dancer trod on my new mobile and broke it (I told Prancer not to give her those stilettos), without you publicizing my tiny indiscretion to all and sundry. Kindly remove your ridiculous offer and make sure it doesn't get to the publisher. This really is too bad.

3 January

Dear Barbara

I received your request for Christmas presents last month, but obtaining the gifts you asked for has proven decidedly difficult. I thought your desire to dedicate a large section of land to wildlife was most noble. However, I couldn't connect it with either of the items you requested in your letter.

First of all you asked if you could have some 'fox gloves'. I wasn't sure how this fitted into the conservation plan, and I'm afraid I couldn't locate any of our Arctic fox neighbours, (they were out at a local watercolour exhibition when I called) so I had to visit our local solicitors, Husky, Husky & Cub. The senior partner has been kind enough to give me some old golfing gloves he doesn't need any more. I hope they're suitable for the fox, and that s/he doesn't mind the fact that they're second-hand – or should I say 'second-paw'? Ho ho!

Anyway, back to your letter; the other thing on your list was some 'Shepherd's Purse'. This turned out to be extremely troublesome; eventually I found a shepherd (he was here on a Splendours of the North Pole package tour) and I asked if he'd give me his purse, but he thought I was trying to mug him and called the police. I have spent the last forty-eight hours in a small cell (there was a delay in

Continued...

~ 2 ~

releasing me because my idiot secretary attempted to pay my bail money with chocolate coins), and have still not managed to obtain the article you wanted. Rather than risk being arrested again, I am sending you my own purse, and suggest that you use the money in it to help set up your wildlife area *on your own* as it is not a cause I feel I can support you in any further.

Yours, feeling quite overwrought

Father Christmas

PS – I hope the fox gloves fit.

Oops – disaster! You remember that angry letter I sent to Mr Noah? Seems I got hold of the wrong end of the archaic staff.

Send an apology straightaway; I fear that even I can't abuse biblical icons and get away with it.

5 January

Dear Mr Noah

I have to say that letters like yours make me very angry. I know we live in an age where the consumer can order anything, usually on credit. (Indeed, Vixen recently ran up an enormous Visa card bill by purchasing a number of Connoisseur Ruminant Hampers on E-hay.) I do realise, too, that no guidelines are published regarding the items you can 'order', if you like, from me.

However, I do expect people to exercise a little self-control. I was irritated to see that not only is your list of requests extremely long, but I also notice that everything has been ordered *in duplicate*. This really is unacceptable. I have to say I find this endless kneeling to the god of consumerism quite distasteful.

As for your gibberish about 'rainbows', 'olive branches' and 'floods', I'm afraid I couldn't make head or tail of it. I'm sorry, Mr Noah, but I refuse to feed this horrible modern hunger of yours for material possessions. It simply isn't the right way to survive life's storms.

Yours, not anticipating any resultant biblical catastrophes whatsoever

Father Christmas

Tinsel, I said letters that made me look intelligent; I don't want people to read about my mistakes. And why aren't you back from your lunch break yet? Look, it turns out that I'm going to have to go away for a week or so. There's been a problem at one of our toy factories based in Barbados, so I'm going to have to leave you in charge while I sort it all out. Really bad luck for me, having to endure a week of sun, sea, and union disputes, but it can't be helped.

Anyway, it means you'll have to prepare the next pages of the book on your own. Do you think you're ready for that kind of responsibility? Get Sparkles and Attrina and the rest of the team to help you. We're going to need all wings on deck. Hopefully, even with your lowly female brain, you can manage to find some letters showing my mental powers at their most acute. And one tiny matter: as it's January, the returned gifts are arriving thick and fast, so you'll need to deal with the Bath Oil Slick which seems to have formed in the basement thanks to all those unwanted bottles that leaked when Comet sat on them. You'll also need to clear away the Sock Mountain, and the clouds of talcum powder currently causing that partial eclipse. So there'll be plenty to keep you out of mischief while I'm gone. As they say: the devil makes work for idle wings. Incidentally, have you seen my suntan lotion? I may need it for these business meetings.

6 January

Dear Roy

I received your note this morning and it has perplexed me a great deal. I can understand why you suspect me of removing a piece of jigsaw from the puzzle you were doing on Christmas Eve (thereby thoughtlessly making it impossible for you to complete it on Christmas morning), but honestly, I didn't touch the puzzle; I barely went near it.

I do recall visiting your house and seeing the puzzle on the table, and I remember noticing the picture on the box: 'Mole Tunnelling in Darkness'. But I certainly didn't move any pieces; in fact I had to restrain myself from doing so – as I leant over, for a closer look, I saw how two of the sections could be fitted together, but I didn't think it was my place to interfere.

I'm sorry I can't help you to shed any light on this mystery. I'm afraid you'll have to remain in total darkness, rather like the unfinished mole.

Yours, feeling very puzzled*

Father Christmas

* You'll have to forgive my little pun, but I am well known in the office for my sense of humour. So much so, in fact, that my secretary described me the other day as 'one big joke'. She does have her good points, sometimes.

Sparkles, I'm going to use FC's office as my base while he's away. Could you get the stationery order sorted while I reorganise the filing system?

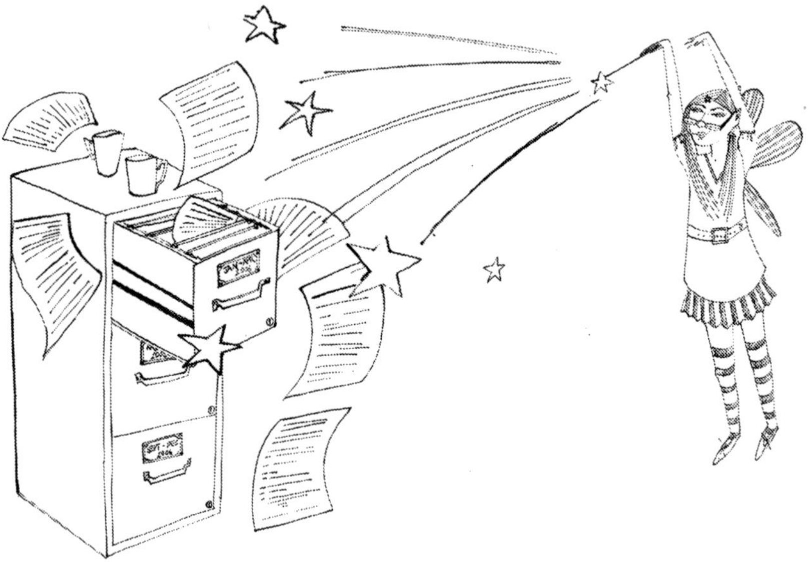

I've arranged for the decorators to come in later in the week. Responses to the staff questionnaire on colour preferences should be in by then; I e-mailed it to everyone half an hour ago. If the minutes of the meeting with the Dwarf Social Committee are ready I'll check them and we can issue them. I loved Jingle's idea about an annual staff Charity Ball; perhaps you could do some preliminary costings? Remember to consult some of the younger dwarfs (say, the under-nineties) when you start exploring band choices. Let me know if there's any news on the Wrapping Paper Design Contest – thanks. – Tinsel

Dear Tinsel

Arrived here at the airport and realised you'd forgotten to pack my passport in the correct compartment of my briefcase. Tut tut. Luckily the friendly airport staff recognised me from my pictures, and after a brief 72-hour wait in a custody cell, the discovery of my passport, and an absolute minimum of police brutality, I was allowed to continue with my journey.

I'll write again when I land.

Father Christmas

PS Remember to feed the walrus. He's my new pet; not sure if I mentioned him before I set off?

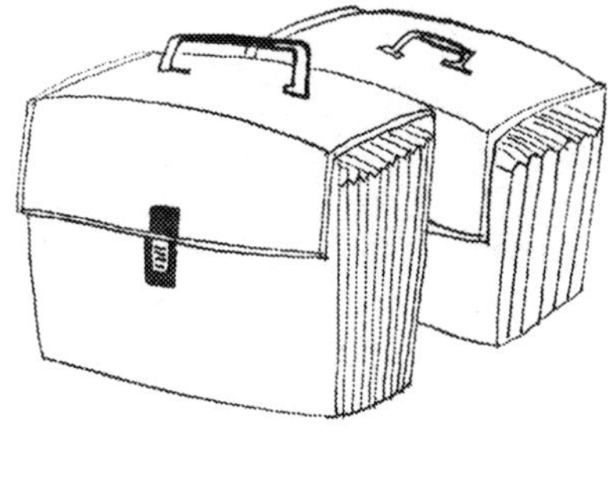

8 January

Dear Ms Langdon

My dry cleaning was delivered to me yesterday, along with your somewhat impertinent note, in which you alleged that it was impossible to remove the soot from the artificial white fur trim on my jacket. This is simply not acceptable, Ms Langdon; I cannot possibly wear the jacket in its current state and the fact that I 'operate in the dark', as you point out, cuts no ice with me whatsoever. I am sending my jacket back to you and expect all of the soot to have been removed before it is returned. Then, and only then, will I pay your (frankly exorbitant) bill.

Yours indignantly

Father Christmas

PS As well as my other sources of dissatisfaction, I am also appalled that your staff seemingly allow foreign bodies to adhere to clothes as they are being cleaned. For example, I discovered the enclosed piece of black, soggy misshapen cardboard hidden under the sleeve of my jacket; I have no idea where it came from.

Sparkles, please arrange for transportation of FC's walrus back to whatever sanctuary he obtained it from – I suspect it was Walrus Wonderland, but you'd better check. Make sure you send them a large donation towards its upkeep taken from his private savings (try the stash he keeps behind the portrait of his mother in his office). Also, get Kristabella to authorise an immediate audit of the soft toy warehouse and of the board games' storage unit. Results to me, please, together with an analysis of projected profit margins and staffing requirements.

Drinks after work with the pixies from Packing? See you at the HSB at 6. – Tinsel

Dear Tinsel

Landed after a rather nerve-racking flight. I knew it was a mistake to bring the reindeer. They really don't make good passengers, but the pilot could have been more understanding when they tried to lift everyone's spirits by singing carols over the loudspeaker system. Anyway, I hope the book is going well. These high-level negotiations are keeping me pretty busy. I'm a vital figure at the meetings so I won't have much time for writing; you'll have to cope as best you can alone. Within the next ten minutes, for instance, I have to decide on the wine-choice for my table at lunch – that's the sort of responsibility they're prepared to entrust me with.

Good luck with struggling on without my helpful words of wisdom ...

Father Christmas

PS How's my walrus doing?

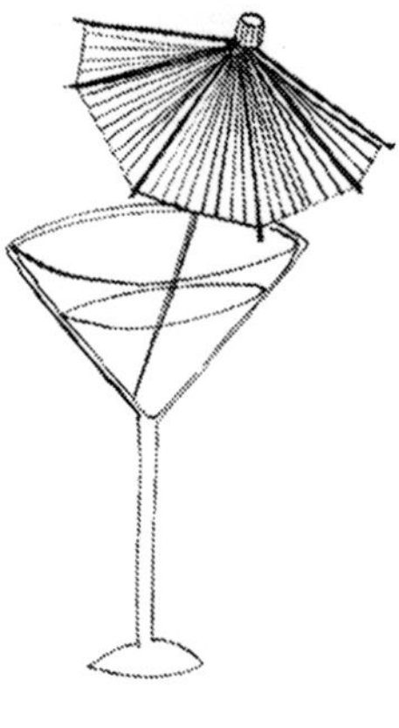

10 January

Dear Mr Filchett

Thank you for your letter; it was lovely to hear from somebody with such a genuine interest in the job that I do. You say that your own line of work is fairly similar; apparently we both enter houses silently at night without the owner's knowledge. What a coincidence. It's such a small world, I always say.

You ask about one of the houses that I visited last year in your area; as you say you're planning to visit it soon too, and want to be prepared so that you can do a really 'professional job'. The house you mention belongs to a couple called the Pryke-Joneses, but I wouldn't bother with trying to talk to them too much, if I were you. I seem to remember they're rather stand-offish; just because they own all those expensive paintings and lots of valuable jewellery, they seem to think that they're above everyone else. It's as if they believe that the rest of us are either blindingly stupid or else out to rob them. And it's not as if having that huge safe hidden behind the Gainsborough in the hall is going to fool any self-respecting burglar anyway. Better to go in, do what you need to do, and leave quickly rather than staying to chat. I'm sure that they'll appreciate your discretion.

Yours helpfully

Father Christmas

Sparkles, can you confirm that the walrus is back at the sanctuary? Sorry it took you so long to find FC's little horde; I'd forgotten how many portraits of his mother he has in his office.

Have the fairies made a decision yet about the proposed new ice hockey facilities? No need to get written responses from them – a show of wings should be sufficient.

Hopefully everyone has signed Twinkle's card ready for his birthday later this week? I think we'll need some more donations towards Holly's retirement gift. Make sure you get a contribution from FC, either use same stash as before or you could try the coins he has hidden in the toe of his spare left boot.

Cinema tonight with Attrina and co? I think Ice Age *is on if you fancy a home movie. – Tinsel*

Dear Tinsel

Alas I will not be returning yet, as an extra-long meeting has given me a severe case of sunburn – the price I have to pay for being such a workaholic, I'm afraid.

I certainly haven't been lying around outside without sufficient SF30 on, whatever the reindeer tell you.

See you soon

Father Christmas

PS Does my walrus miss me, do you think? Tell him I've bought him an 'I ♥ Barbados' T-shirt. I've also written him a poem which I've forwarded, so that you can pin it on the office notice board after you've read it aloud to him. I'm sure everyone will find it very moving.

FC's Poem

I wandered lonely as a walrus
That swims forlornly out at sea
When all at once I saw a crowd
Of penguins staring straight at me
Beside the cliffs, upon the ice
Their faces were not very nice.

Continuous as the chimney tops
That pour their smoke into the sky,
There was an awful lot of them
And I was forced to wonder why:
A plot, perhaps, hatched secretly,
To undermine unlucky me.

The waves were blue and cold but they
Were colder still in look and eye
A poet would quite nervous feel
If crowds of them came strolling by
I gazed and gazed with fearful pen
Hoping we would not meet again.

Yet when on my settee I sit
Not really thinking much at all
They barge their way into my mind
And make me feel extremely small
And then my heart with terror squeaks
And tries to flee their nasty beaks.

13 January

Dear Mr Wolf

I must say that I was most displeased to have the presents I left for you last Christmas (one bulldozer, one heat-resistant waterproof suit) returned to me this morning. Both items had clearly been used and were not in particularly good condition. It has taken a team of elves five hours to clear the straw and twigs out of the bulldozer driver's cab (they also found a Meat Loaf tape, and one or two bricks).

I went to a great deal of trouble to obtain your presents, Mr Wolf, and it is upsetting for me to have them returned without any sort of explanation. Your letter seems to me to be total gibberish – what is 'Mad Pig Disease', anyway? I hope that you will exhibit a great deal more gratitude in the future.

Yours, still feeling quite angry, actually

Father Christmas

Hi again, Sparkles. FC stuck in Barbados, so at least I can sort out things here a bit more. Rudolph phoned earlier. The reindeer have all been homesick, except for Dancer, who has been sick because she had too many pina coladas.

I've been updating the computer system so that we can stocktake electronically – should save hours, and it will mean the goblins can focus on quality control, which should please them. We've still got all the returned gifts to deal with, but I really feel we should donate the lot to charity, preferably before FC returns and tries to insist we wrap them up and send them out as next year's presents.

The most popular choice for the new office décor seems to be iced fern, so can you get the decorators to make a start tomorrow? I'll be away from my phone for a while as our Senior Welfare Imp has identified a problem: the pixies tying the bows on the parcels are starting to show signs of

Repetitive Strain Injury, and I need to look into it as a matter of urgency. The last thing we need is another costly gift-wrapping disaster like last year's Scissor Hands fiasco.

See you later – Tinsel

Dear Tinsel

Nearly recovered from my sunburn now but I'm still trying my best not to overdo it – don't want to give myself a relapse. Luckily the union dispute seems to have been resolved in my absence – doubtless due to the sterling groundwork I put in before I was so unexpectedly stricken. So I'm trying to sit by the pool slightly more now, building my exertion levels up gradually.

Back soon, don't worry.

Father Christmas

PS No 'thank you' note for the T-shirt or poem yet, I notice?

16 January

Dear Ms Stewart, aka Ms Hallowe'en 1983

Your letter arrived too late for Christmas (I wouldn't trust Penguin Post again if I were you), but in plenty of time for next year. My secretary, unfortunately, spilt some red wine on it. Such a clumsy fairy she is, a real butter-wings. You simply can't get the mythical entities these days. Anyway, most of your letter escaped intact; it was only the final sentence, which began 'If you fail me in any of these requests …' which was washed away by the Merlot. I expect you'd gone on to write something like 'I'll understand completely', though, so I won't worry about it.

Your request for a cauldron is easily dealt with; I've selected a nice big casserole dish (khaki with attractive fruit motif) from our oven-to-table cookware range, and it's being wrapped for you in seasonal paper (khaki with attractive star motif) even as I write this. The cat that you wanted should pose no problem either, and I salute your organisational skills in having chosen its name already. I can picture you now, standing on your doorstep every evening and summoning little Beelzebub. What a charming scene.

Finally, you have asked for a broomstick. A very morally wholesome choice, if I may say so. I find that many women/fairies rely on machines to do their house/grottowork for them these days, and often they're not prepared to accept anything connected with homemaking as a Christmas gift.

Continued…

~ 2 ~

There was once an unpleasant scene even here, in my very own office, just because I decided that Tinsel could do with a new scrubbing brush as her Yuletide present. She flew at me - literally - and started scrubbing my face with it, shrieking that the first unpleasant item she intended to get rid of was my 'smug expression'. I managed to promise her a purple Volkswagen Beetle seconds before my skin surrendered its protective coating of beard, and she stopped, but that moment is still painfully etched in the darkest, non-glitter-coated reaches of my long-term memory.

Tinsel spent the rest of the day driving drunken gnomes and elves to our office for a colossal party; I spent the rest of the day nursing my raw skin and trying to ignore the roars of the Beetle and its inebriated passengers. I really hope that you have a much better Christmas than I did, Ms Stewart. At least no-one will be asking you to change things into Beetles.

Yours sincerely

Father Christmas

Hi Sparkles. The new colour scheme looks great – loads of positive feedback from staff already. Your suggestion about starting a workplace crèche is excellent. We could easily convert FC's library – he never uses it anyway – especially now we have the decorators in. Let's proceed with it immediately; your preliminary report was very thorough, and I don't really see how we can continue without one. Star and some of the other pixies have already expressed an interest in staffing it, and we have plenty of toys to stock it with, so let's aim to get it up and running before FC returns.

We can provide in-service training for those who need it, and there's a team of Magical Infant-Care Professionals standing by to help.

Can't get to the HSB tonight – loads of paperwork to catch up on thanks to you-know-who. But buy Twinkle a birthday acorn juice on me, and hopefully I'll get this lot cleared within a few hours. Then I'll probably go home, have a hot bath, and curl up in front of Buffy the Vampire Sleigher. *Ring me later if you get the chance? – Tinsel*

Dear Tinsel

Just taking a break from packing to write you another letter, as I want to be supportive – I can imagine how difficult it's been, struggling on without me. The good news is I'll be home soon, so you'll be able to put your wings up and relax while I take back the reins (ho ho). The bad news is that my ungrateful walrus STILL hasn't sent me a thank you note. I'm beginning to think he doesn't deserve an owner like me and we should send him back to that walrus sanctuary while we have the chance.

See you tomorrow.

Father Christmas

19 January

Dear Mr Axel

I was deeply interested in your proposal to open the Santa's Grotto at your department store slightly earlier this year – July, I think you said? This is a particularly excellent idea because it coincides with what would normally be my off-peak season, so I could certainly make the daily appearances you require without compromising my other responsibilities.

You express concern that there may not be room for as much Christmas merchandise as usual because of the summer stock, but I'm sure we can use it to our advantage. For instance the boules could be covered in cotton wool to represent snowballs, and any leftover tents could perhaps be transformed into igloos. This would certainly put you ahead of your rival department stores, where Christmas displays often appear as late as August, or, in a few cases, September.

I would like to reassure you that I don't see your extension of the yuletide season as anything other than an obliging attempt to spread my workload more evenly throughout the year – certainly not the 'transparent attempt at hideously greedy commercialism' that my secretary dismissed it as. Some fairies are too cynical for their own good, I'm afraid.

Yours, as clear-sightedly as always

Father Christmas

Sparkles, FC is back tomorrow, so we'll need to ensure all loose ends are tied up by then. Crèche looks brilliant. The baby goblins love the new drum set, and the young dwarves seem to be enjoying the toy pickaxes.

Thanks to the electronic stocktake, I've managed to avoid ordering 10,000 unnecessary jars of bath salts, so hopefully we should get fewer complaints this year.

The elves are very excited about your plans for turning the disused North-facing attic into an Art Gallery, and they've invited us out for drinks to celebrate. We'll chill out at the HSB till 7, then we're moving on to the theatre. The sea-lions are performing their Amateur Aquatic Production of The Ice Man Cometh, *if you're interested? – Tinsel*

Dear Tinsel

We landed safely and I'm just taking the opportunity to write you a final letter while the reindeer get the luggage fastened to the sleigh. That ungrateful walrus hasn't sent me the smallest acknowledgement of all my kind wishes. It's almost as if nobody bothered to sit for two hours a day at the edge of his icy rock pool to read my letters aloud to him. I'm afraid he's ruined his chances of staying with me, anyway – I'd like you to send him back to that sanctuary I bought him from. A pet is for Christmas, thank goodness, and not for life.

I'll see you soon. After all these top level, skilful negotiations, it will be a relief to return to your simpler, more mundane level of thinking.

Father Christmas

30 January

Dear Dr Chang

I see from your headed writing paper that you are a psychotherapist, and I demand to know straightaway why you're writing to me. What is this, an unofficial preliminary assessment by letter, or something? The whole business is quite outrageous. There is absolutely nothing wrong with my mind; it is completely normal, and if any of those polar bears have been secretly claiming otherwise, I'll prosecute them for libel, or slander, or whatever it is called when huge white fluffy creatures say nasty things about you. They're always doing it, every time I see them; lots of them can't look me in the eye any more because they feel so guilty about attacking me behind my back.

Anyway, what has any of this got to do with you? What right do you have to start asking me questions about polar bears? I notice you don't give away any of your innermost secrets in your letter. Oh no, the only thing you say is that you'd like a large dark green vase for your wife's Christmas present. No damaging implications to be extracted from that, I see; no mention there of polar bears or furtive whisperings or frosty looks being exchanged behind igloos.

Continued...

~ 2 ~

I have to say I find these devious and underhand tactics of yours completely distasteful, and I can only assume that you've been talking to penguins. I don't know what you think you're trying to prove, but you've picked the wrong person to tangle with. You won't find a more normal man than me anywhere at the North Pole, and if you suggest otherwise I shall get the incredibly gifted husky I use as a solicitor to sue you for every penny you've got. I hope I make myself clear? That is to say, I hope you understand me; I didn't mean that I'd like to become transparent. Only mad people would want that, and I'm completely sane.

Yours, still in full control of my facilities, thank you

Father Christmas

Tinsel! What on earth has been going on here? I returned to find the office in complete chaos. Is this the result of your silly, new-fangled, wings-on approach? Not only do the pixies formerly responsible for wrapping presents now seem to be wearing fancy dress and chanting Ring-a-Ring-of-Edelweiss *with a group of spritelets, but when I opened the door to my library I found a playpen full of drum-wielding baby goblins singing at the tops of their voices. As if that wasn't enough, the office appears to have been repainted in some unpleasant green hue, not nearly as attractive as that fetching shade, 'hint of kippered herring', I chose myself twenty-five years ago. This is too much. I'm so furious that nothing, no, not even a timely authorial sleight of hand involving the offer of a knighthood from the Queen herself, will save you from a compulsory golden wingshake.*

* * *

It's happened. My dreams realised after all these years. A timely authorial sleight of hand involving the offer of a knighthood from the Queen herself. We must make sure my reply is absolutely perfect. Tinsel, I suggest that we let bygones be bygones. I'll definitely need you to lend a wing.

February

1 February

Dear Ma'am

I received your letter less than thirty seconds ago, and am endeavouring to reply to it as rapidly as possible, not wanting to cause you any inconvenience whatsoever. *[Put in another grovelly sentence here, Tinsel; something about being gratified to receive etc. etc.]*

I feel extremely flattered that you are considering the possibility of including me in next year's Honours List. I will certainly endeavour to do as you suggest and try to attract the sort of positive publicity necessary to secure such a special privilege.

I remain, Ma'am, your obedient humble servant

Father Christmas

Tinsel! This is it, my chance at last. Let me start by putting on another Carol Service for the old folk. I know they had one a few weeks ago, but we could call this an Early Bird Special so they don't realise it's the same songs. That should earn me a few royal brownie points, don't you think? Meanwhile back to more worthy matters – that celebrity photographer, for instance.

5 February

Dear Wilfred

Thank you for your letter; I will certainly be able to supply you with the camera equipment you require. I expect that as a keen photographer you are always seeking to improve your own performance, so I am even prepared to offer myself as a model in order to help you achieve photographic perfection.

You could, for example, take a dramatic shot of me landing on the roof with my sleigh, and I'd be happy to keep circling and landing until you were satisfied you'd got a good picture. Then I could pose for a portrait, with the out-of-focus chimney in the background. (You wouldn't mind a spot of nocturnal ladder-climbing, I'm sure; it's all in the name of Art.) If you balanced on the top of the chimney and pointed the camera downwards, you could get an extremely unusual camera angle, with the top of my hat just visible as I disappeared out of sight. Then you could do an action shot of me landing in the fireplace (my secretary cleverly suggested lighting a fire there to make it more dramatic), and next a close-up of me filling one of your stockings.

Incidentally, if any of my reindeer get in touch asking you to photograph them, please refuse kindly but firmly. Media attention of any sort isn't good for them; Rudolph became quite impossible one year when his nose became the unlikely focus of a Christmas song, and Vixen recently head-butted a local reporter just because she claimed that the article he wrote about her wasn't flattering enough.

Continued....

~ 2 ~

The sleigh will certainly be too full to carry any oversized egos on board. In any case, you will need all the film you've got to take pictures of me.

Yours, with his best side pointed fetchingly towards the camera

Father Christmas

Tinsel, which is *my best side? It's so hard to choose.*

8 February

Dear Ms Boylan

It is with great pleasure that I'm informing you that I've invited my hand-picked choir, the Carolling Fairies, to visit your establishment once more. I realise that this will be their second visit in ten weeks, but as I always say when gift-wrapping thermal socks, you can't have too much of a good thing. Would two o'clock on the 12th be acceptable? I hope you (and your residents, of course) won't have any objection if a film crew shows up to record some of the proceedings.

It's just that - between you and me - I'm trying to impress somebody Quite High Up at the moment, and some positive publicity of this nature ('Father Christmas Sends Fairies to Cheer Up Old Folks in Their Hour of Need') would look quite impressive on the front page of *The Icicle*, and may help a great deal. I trust that will be alright with you? I wouldn't want you to think I was exploiting your organisation to create flattering photo opportunities to show myself in a good light.

I'm sure that you will enjoy this year's concert a great deal. Our choir has really grown in number, ever since the refreshments contract was given to our local off-licence, in fact.

Anyway, I believe this month's programme is completely new, and I'm confident your residents will be riveted by what is on offer. I believe some of them found it so relaxing last time, they actually went to sleep.

Continued...

~ 2 ~

I very much look forward to hearing your account of how it all goes, and, hopefully, watching the event itself on national television.

Yours altruistically

Father Christmas

Better start tuning up the old vocal chords, eh, Tinsel? And make sure you arrange for lots of applause in all the right places; it may be best if you get some of your friends to clap their wings loudly at the end of every song.

9 February

Dear Frosty (Jr.)

I don't know whether you thought I was going to be impressed by a description of yourself as an 'aspiring snowman', but frankly, I have a complete contempt for those pathetic social climbers who attempt to rise above their station. In fact I think your aspirations to become a snowman are verging on the abominable.

I will not be supplying you with the pipe that you ask for, as I only have one of these and I need to keep it for my own use, in case the no-smoking ban in our office ever gets lifted. The carrot you request is a possibility, but frankly I don't think I'd ever get it past the reindeer in one piece, so I think it's best to leave it, rather than to stir up potential trouble. Their squabbles last year over the various chocolates people left lying around were very wearing; I seem to recall one particularly vicious disagreement over a box of Fairy Milk.

I've got to close now as I have to prepare a flask of something non-alcoholic to take with me on the sleigh tonight. My secretary has banned me from enjoying any of the sherry I get offered at people's houses – she says it's dangerous to drink and fly – and she's got a do-it-yourself breathalyser kit lined up to test me with when I

Continued…

~ 2 ~

arrive back at the office, so I suppose I'd better do as she says. In any case, I'm trying to cultivate a particularly spotless reputation at the moment, as I have people to please, places to go, and ambitions to fulfil. I'm certainly far too busy to waste any time in furthering the interests of a would-be upwardly mobile collection of snowflakes.

Yours, feeling it's every (snow)man for himself

Father Christmas

There, Tinsel, that's sent him packing. I don't like turning a cold shoulder, (ho ho!) but if there's one thing I can't stand it's pretentiousness ...

Where's that letter to Mrs Fenworthy, by the way? Such affability. Such charm. Such expensive writing paper.

9 February

Dear Mrs Fenworthy

Thank you for your letter, written on that delightful caviar-scented writing paper. So much classier, I'm sure you're right, than the ostentatious personalised paper used by your next-door neighbour, Mrs Jones. Regarding the presents you request, I should easily be able to find you an antique revolver (far older and more illegal than the one you spotted through the window on Mrs Jones's table) as well as the full-length fur coat (better quality than hers, and made from a species that is much more endangered).

Like you, dear lady, I feel it is one's moral duty to better oneself whenever possible.

Yours, with one albino chamois leather boot planted firmly on the social ladder

Father Christmas

Tinsel! This is an emergency. Bring my writing pad – quick. I think it's tucked under my Homemade Cocktail recipe for 'Bloody Fairies'.

11 February

Dear Ms Boylan

I received your letter this morning after watching the Carolling Fairies on the *Nine o'clock News* last night, so I suppose I was prepared for what it contained, although I didn't expect you to be quite so angry. I can only apologise. I had no idea that the Gothic Goblins would turn up with the Carolling Fairies and set up that huge system of amplifiers and microphones and then put on a concert that could be heard five miles away.

Believe me, I was as surprised as you were. I have no idea how they learned to play all that Glenn Miller dance music, and it was unfortunate, as you say, that one of the Carolling Fairies locked you in the laundry room so that the residents had the chance to use the phone in your office to ring their friends and invite them to turn up as well. Two thousand people must have been quite a squeeze. And I can understand your annoyance at not having been released from the laundry room for over eight hours.

I very much hope that you'll decide *not* to sue me, although I can understand the temptation is fairly strong. I would, of course, be taking the strongest disciplinary measures against the offending fairies and goblins, had the entire staff not threatened me with a forty-eight hour walkout if I'd imposed any sort of punishment on the parties concerned. Needless to say, I will certainly pay you compensation for the damage done to the lid of your piano; who would have thought that seven octogenarians could have been so agile?

Continued...

~ 2 ~

I can only apologise again for the distress that this unfortunate incident has caused, and hope that the trigger-happy 76-year-old with the water cannon can be persuaded to surrender his weapon peacefully. I'm glad the fact that my reputation has been damaged beyond repair enables you to feel that justice has at least been done.

Yours, in humble acquiescence

Father Christmas

Tinsel? What have you done with the promotional video that PR firm sent me? I want to watch it again; the woman on there is really impressive. I found the crazed, demonic glint in her eye rather off-putting at first, but Vixen told me it's this year's must-have accessory for PR specialists. Apparently they won't leave their Canary Wharf Three-bedroom Lairs without it.

13 February

Dear Eva Dell

Thank you for the special promotional video, which arrived last week. I'd never considered hiring a public relations firm up until now, but my image has been sadly tarnished by recent events, and if you could help with the damage limitation necessary to restore my former high status, then it would certainly be worth my while to pay your (frankly exorbitant) fee.

I would definitely like to hire your services and am prepared to be totally open about my 'real aspirations', just as your introductory leaflet demands. Let me start, then, by saying that my main desire is to be given a you-know-what by you-know-who in the you-know-what in the you-know-when. Now I can't put it more plainly than that, can I?

Yours sincerely

Father Christmas

Tinsel, I am most annoyed. I thought that since it's Shrove Tuesday you'd be only too happy to whip up a few industrial-sized pancakes for the reindeer and me. Our hopes were high, cutlery poised; a few wisps of smoke appeared promisingly from the direction of the kitchen, and what happened? It eventually transpired that you'd simply put your wand onto 'char' setting and had viciously incinerated my favourite wooden spoon! Have you ever tried breaking it to a roomful of teary-eyed ruminants that their dreams are doomed to disappointment? I don't think anyone understands how tough my job really is.

14 February

Dear Antonio

Thank you for your reminder card regarding my visit to your salon, and for your promotional leaflet. It is certainly reassuring to note that beard extensions in assorted colours will be available soon at reasonable prices; also that I will be able to try out your new 'glitter perm' within the next few weeks if I so choose.

Unfortunately I don't seem to have a free slot in my diary at the moment, what with all the madcap social activities going on here, but will get in touch as soon as I do. By the way, please alert me if Rudolph contacts you again about having his nose pierced. I think the whole business has been resolved now, but I just want to make sure. Also, Dancer wants me to confirm with you that she will 'have the silver highlights done on the 16th', whatever that means.

Carefree snipping,

Father Christmas

Tinsel, I'd like you to contact the Post Office to find out what has happened to today's delivery. I know you received your 48 envelopes and 17 bunches of flowers safely, but my portion of today's mail seems to have mysteriously gone astray. Apart from the reminder from the salon, all that arrived for me was a heart-shaped card in my mother's handwriting that said 'Never mind, dear, at least you've done well in your career'. Surely there must be some mistake? Check to see whether the mail has been delayed by frozen leaves on the model railway line, would you?

24 February

Dear Eva Dell

Thank you for your fascinating leaflet, *Outline of Devious Initiatives Guaranteed to Boost Popularity and Restore a Damaged Reputation to its Former Glory*. Its author certainly seemed to know what he was talking about, although I'm not sure that signing himself TB was the best idea, squeaky cleanness-wise.

Your idea of creating a grotto in a public place and distributing presents free of charge – aided, as you say, by a team of aesthetically pleasing fairies and gnomes – was really superb.

Obviously a grotto in an impoverished inner-city area would be best from a publicity angle, but I am somewhat concerned about the nature of the clientèle such a locality may attract, and would like to suggest Knightsbridge as an alternative.

Continued...

~ 2 ~

We should be safe there from the illiterate rabble, and if anyone does cause trouble I'll get the fairies to call the police and have them removed. I know Christmas is meant to be for everybody but there are limits!

I thought I'd position a gnome at the front, checking the financial credentials of the client – if the accompanying adult doesn't have an Antarctica Express Gold Card, then the child will be turned away.

Successful candidates will be led through a short passageway (suitably festooned with fairy lights and artificial snow) into the actual grotto, where I will greet them with my Festive Cheery Laugh supplied with Matching Handshake.

After the toy has been selected, and unwrapped with appropriate expressions of gratitude and delight, the gnome will lead the child out of a concealed back exit, unless they look like photo-opportunity material – if they're on crutches, for instance.

Thank you for your inspired idea. I thought perhaps I should start practising my new signature…

Yours sincerely

Sir Christmas

It has a pleasant ring to it, does it not? Tinsel, my claret, in the crystal decanter, if you please.

26 February

Most Honoured Highness

I was gratified to receive your letter two and a half minutes ago; words alone can hardly do justice to the honour I esteem it to receive this sort of attention from a person of your rank.

I humbly agree with everything you wrote in your letter, your Highness. I am completely unfitted for any sort of privilege or reward, and following yesterday's 'Embarrassing Escapade in Naughty Knightsbridge' (as *The Daily Snow* called it) I would certainly not expect you to look favourably on any petition on my behalf, now or at any time in the future, begging you to resurrect those golden hopes I once entertained.

If only more than one child had been eligible to enter my grotto. And if only she hadn't whispered that she was disappointed at meeting Tinsel rather than an 'A List' celebrity fairy like Tinkerbell ... And if only Tinsel hadn't heard her, flown into a temper, and hit her over the head with her wand, and if only the onlooking children hadn't joined in, as well as all the other fairies, gnomes, and parents. And if only the whole thing hadn't ended in a savage, undignified brawl ... Thank goodness, as you say, that the road sweeper was there and was able to take control of the situation.

What can I say, your Highness? How can I apologise enough for this unprecedented shock to your royal sensibilities? I am as dust, I am an earwig; I am less than

Continued...

~ 2 ~

the ant on which you may (accidentally) set your royal foot. Alas! The name of Christmas has been forever blotted in your eyes. This is truly the winter of my discontent.

Farewell, O noble one; I shall ask you to sicken yourself no longer by gazing at the filthy ramblings of this defiled minion's undeserving pen.

I remain, Ma'am, your obedient humble servant

Father Christmas

Tinsel, get me some stale bread and stagnant water, please. I'll need something to sustain me: I've spent a painful morning composing insect metaphors. Alas, alack. Unworthy wretch that I am.

29 February

Dear Mr Holmes

I received your impertinent letter this morning, and was most indignant that you should have chosen to use me as a subject for your ridiculous so-called deductions. I am not a 'pitiful, middle-aged no-hoper with an unfashionable beard and a weight problem,' as the first sentence of your ridiculous report on me claims, and I don't care if you and your friend Watson did 'study the evidence remaining from last year's delivery of presents most thoroughly'. Nor that you have 'spent the last ten months compiling a detailed analysis of my character, appearance and past life'. I refuse to allow a nineteenth century nonentity such as yourself to waste any more of my valuable time.

Yours indignantly

Father Christmas

There, Tinsel; that's told him. How dare he claim to know everything about me on the basis of such flimsy evidence? I've a good mind to mock his inadequacies in one of my poems; that will teach him not to tangle with my beard.

My cup of coffee in here please, when you're ready.

* * *

Tinsel! My mother has just phoned to say that she's coming down for the weekend. Can you book her a room at the Happy Sleigh Bell? And tell the reindeer to be on their best behaviour. Perhaps Dancer could stay with her cousins while Mother's here? If she parades around in her Guns'n'Roses harness again we're done for; the last thing we want is for those two to go head to antler.

FC's Poem

O noble hero, burning bright
In the chimneys of the night
What immoral hand or eye
Could make ridiculous deductions about thy
fearful symmetry?

In what distant shrubs or trees
Formed the grandeur of thine knees?
What great mountains did thou climb
To make thy muscles so sublime?

And what bulging toy-filled sack
Could full accessorise thy back?
How to match thy scarlet suit?
With what red glove? And what black boot?

What fur-trimmed hat could full encase
The source of all thy wit and grace?
The manly workings of thy brain -
What beard could such largesse sustain?

When the elves threw down their tools
Their task complete, their sweat in pools:
Did he smile their work to see?
Did he give them cake for tea?

O noble hero, burning bright,
In the chimneys of the night:
What immoral hand or eye,
Could make ridiculous deductions about thy
fearful symmetry?

4 March

Dear Bernard

Thank you for your letter and fascinating list of presents. I like my correspondents to have a sense of humour, and chuckled heartily at your joke about 'doing me in' if I didn't 'come up with the goods'.

I'll certainly be able to manage the plastic swords, toy guns and water pistols that you asked for, and may I take this opportunity of congratulating you on your pleasantly masculine choice of presents? I expect that when you grow up you're hoping to go into some exciting, male-dominated career area, like boxing, or foxhunting, or armed robbery. Splendid, Bernard! I always say, 'boys should be boys'.

Yours approvingly

Father Christmas

Tinsel! Mother found some old letters I've been really late replying to, and she's insisted I send these people telegrams straightaway. I tried to tell her that no-one uses telegrams these days but she wouldn't listen – you know how stubborn females can be. The only thing is, it's snowing, and Mother won't allow me to go out, so could you possibly take them to the village? Dancer could pull you on the small sledge if you like; you know I wanted her out of the way as much as possible this weekend. If Mother catches a glimpse of her antler-stud, I'll never hear the last of it.

Also, while you're there, perhaps you could get me some money from the cash point? Fifteen silver pieces from my savings account at the Glistening Bank should be sufficient.

DEAR LEONARDO STOP CANVAS AND EASEL ON THEIR WAY STOP THIS MOANER WOMAN SOUNDS A BIT HALF-HEARTED STOP WHY NOT CHOOSE A MODEL WITH A REAL SMILE? STOP BETTER LUCK NEXT TIME, EH? STOP
– F. CHRISTMAS

DEAR MISS HAVISHAM STOP YOU SAY YOU WANT A NICELY BRONZED CHIPPENDALE TO REPLACE YOUR WIMPISH FIANCÉ STOP DON'T REALLY SEE HOW A PIECE OF FURNITURE WILL BE A SUBSTITUTE STOP WAS YOUR FIANCÉ PARTICULARLY WOODEN? STOP HAPPY CHRISTMAS ANYWAY STOP
– F. CHRISTMAS

DEAR JULIET STOP SLEEPING DRAUGHT ON ITS WAY STOP CHECK THAT ROMEO KNOWS WHAT YOU'RE DOING STOP
– F. CHRISTMAS

DEAR MRS MACBETH STOP HAVE DISPATCHED SOAP AS REQUESTED STOP GUARANTEED TO KEEP HANDS SPOTLESS STOP DON'T DO ANYTHING RASH STOP – F. CHRISTMAS

Tinsel, I hope you won't be much longer. The work is piling up here, and I'm having to entertain Mother, which is never easy at the best of times. She sulked because I beat her at Scrabble, so I let her play Blitzen, but Mother won and now he's *sulking. You'd better be back soon, or else!*

---

8 March

Dear Johnny Javier

Thank you for your intriguing proposal to use me as the basis for one of the computer games that your company is currently working on. I have to say I'm rather a stranger to technology, and 'joystick' and 'screen' are not terms that mean a great deal to me.

Continued...

~ 2 ~

Am I right in thinking that the game is designed to be played by one person who controls me, as the central character, as I travel on my sleigh through a number of different 'levels'? As I move through these 'levels' I have to collect presents which can be converted into 'lives' when I reach a certain number - is that correct?

The thing that worries me is that the journey I have to make in order to collect presents seems to be fraught with so much danger. I mean, there's the huge yeti throwing exploding snowballs at me, not to mention the toxic snowflakes. You mention, in your outline, that if one of the snowflakes hits me once, I 'lose health', twice and I 'lose a life'.

Why do I have to lose a *life*, I wonder? Why not something less drastic, like mislaying a button off my jacket, or something like that?

I'm sorry, Johnny, but on reflection this whole enterprise sounds a bit too risky for my liking. I would prefer it if you sought elsewhere for your computer game hero. You really need someone who's a lot more daring than me; someone who's charismatic and doesn't mind taking risks. I'll have a word with my secretary when she gets back and see if she can think of anyone. Sorry I can't be of more help.

Yours sincerely

Father Christmas

Eight hours to send a few telegrams, Tinsel? What kind of fairy story is that? Mother and I are not amused. Now you're finally back (but still not at your desk, I notice), perhaps we can get some work done? Where were you, anyway?

8 March

Dear Mrs Parkin

Thank you for the information pack you sent me and the kind invitation to join your Slimming and Exercise Club. I cannot think where you obtained such a detailed account of my personal statistics in order to produce that impressive document, *Your Obesity – an Individual Profile*, as only myself and my secretary would have access to that kind of privileged information, but it certainly made interesting reading. Surely I do not need to lose quite as much weight as that to achieve my optimum weight/height ratio? How about changing the ratio by making myself taller? I could add a few extra inches to my hat, for instance.

I would like to reassure you that I do have a strong interest in things nutritional. For instance one of our office gnomes had a birthday recently, and he bought cream cakes for everyone. I had declined my eighth cake, in the interests of healthy living, so Tinsel, my secretary, was going to eat it. 'Stop!' I said (I can be quite forceful, you know). 'Think how many calories are in that cake, Tinsel!

Continued...

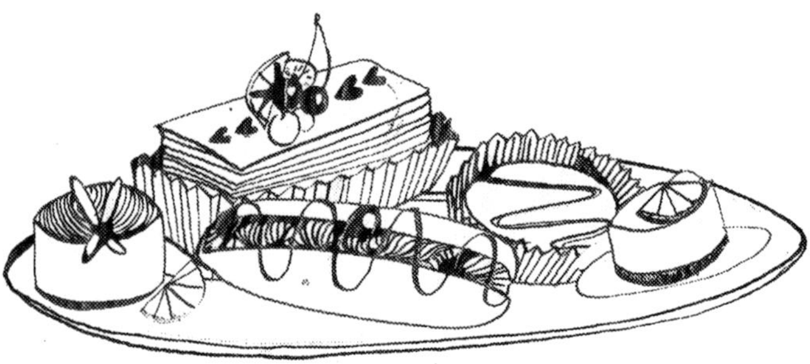

~ 2 ~

Think what it will do to your figure!' Tinsel turned bright red – with shame, I imagine – and then she flung the cake across the room and rushed away.

Unfortunately the cream went all over the documentation I was using to fill in my (Sleigh) Driver's Licence Renewal Form, but at least it was in a good cause … or so I thought at the time. I later caught her eating takeaway pizza with snow-dried tomato topping amid a rowdy group of goblins in the sleigh-bell storeroom, but I thought it best to say nothing. Some fairies never learn, I'm afraid.

I fear I must decline your offer of Free Membership for a Year as I feel that the lifestyle insisted on by your club may be incompatible with the vast amounts of sherry and mince-pies that I am forced to consume in the name of duty. [*Tinsel – get consumption of the above written into my job description immediately. Don't print this*] I wish you and your organisation a very healthy Christmas. Enjoy your free-range stuffing!

Yours sincerely

Father Christmas

I've just had the landlord of the Happy Sleigh Bell on the phone. He's complaining that a couple of customers were being extremely noisy here earlier today. One was a red-headed fairy wearing DMs and the other was a reindeer with her hoof pierced. Any ideas, Tinsel?

9 March

Dear Mrs Hubbard

I received your request for a bone for your dog, but unfortunately, following a rather unpleasant incident last year with a neighbouring farmer, none of our local butchers will supply me with any produce. In fact they are all blaming me because they are about to go out of business. So it's no-go on the bone front, I'm afraid.

Incidentally, Mrs Hubbard, do I detect a note of self-pity in your postscript, where you explain that I won't need to worry about avoiding a fire when I come down your chimney because you can't afford the coal to light one? Are you implying that your OAP Cold Weather Allowance isn't adequate? You know very well you'll receive an extra £2.50 if the temperature stays below minus 15 for twenty consecutive days; what on earth are you complaining about?

Contined...

~2~

I've got to close now because I've got lots of work to be getting on with – not a situation you're familiar with, I'm sure, having retired all those years ago at the age of 75. Apparently, my secretary's just gone off for the day – her second unauthorised absence this week, incidentally – to launch a new computer game. She features in it – well, is the main character, actually – so I've got masses to do, and I certainly haven't got time to waste writing to the likes of you.

Yours in great irritation

Father Christmas

What a day! What with entertaining Mother and making my own coffee, I'm exhausted. In future I would like you to clear all absences with me, in advance, in writing. *Yes, I know you have wings, but that doesn't mean that you can just take off.*

10 March

Dear Julian Rogers

Thanks for your letter, which arrived this morning. I do appreciate a busy director such as yourself taking time out of your schedule to write to me. I'm sorry that you found my performance in your house last year 'disappointing'. I don't have many lines to deliver, as you point out, so it's important I don't mumble those I do have into my beard. 'Speak right out', you say, and I'll try to remember to do it. I'm still working on the jolly laugh.

I did wonder, incidentally, whether there might be any chance of extending my role – I could have an accident with a candlestick maybe, or we could bring on some other characters. I even took the liberty of penning a few scenes myself to show you what the possibilities were. I thought perhaps we could include a musical number or two, as I must say I find the prospect of song-and-dance routines particularly exciting. I even wondered whether we could call the whole production 'Crackers', and I thought that maybe I could perform a big solo number at the end of the first act, with the chorus all dressed up as Christmas stockings, and a dancing fireplace. (I put in a splendid bit of business with a poker). And the lyrics could be so memorable. I thought something along the lines of the following might be acceptable:

Continued…

~ 2 ~

The fire in my heart
Burned out long ago
Then you came down my chimney
And melted my snow

Obviously you're the director, and it's your decision, but if you ask me, 'Crackers' is definitely the way to go.

Yours, hoping for good reviews

Father Christmas

Tinsel, Mother's becoming impossible. She flew into a huge rage just because she discovered I didn't know how to work the tea towel. As if that wasn't enough, she then emptied a cup of acorn juice over my head because she disagreed with my analysis of David Cameron's financial strategies. (I was attempting to prove that he'd got some.) Can't you think of something to keep her busy?

11 March

Dear Mr Swanson

Thank you for your letter. In response to the points raised, let me assure you that every care is taken to check that all the reindeer on my staff are properly provided for. Not only are working hours strictly monitored (and the Reindeer Union Representative quickly alerts me if so much as an antler is raised when it shouldn't be), but in addition, the reindeer are provided with a varied and nutritious diet (a sample menu from The Healthy Antler Canteen is enclosed).

A qualified vet is on standby at all times, and has been involved in the multi-agency approach to reindeer health care that we have recently instigated, whereby each reindeer has a monthly check-up and gets the chance to sit down with the vet and the elf responsible for ruminant husbandry, to discuss his or her physical, mental and social needs. We find that this helps to combat workplace stress – a significant problem among white-collar ruminants, as any sociologist worth his weight in fairy-gold will tell you.

Educational provision is taken seriously, and we were all delighted a couple of months ago when Cupid successfully completed her PhD by producing an 80,000-word thesis entitled *Bonding vs. Exclusion: An In-depth Study of the Adverse Effects of Elitist Sleigh-Pulling Selection Processes on the Individual Psyche and Social Relationships*. I fear that any document containing complicated words such as 'exclusion' and 'study' goes straight over my beard, but Tinsel, my secretary, read it, and even bought its author a vodka on the rocks at the Happy Sleigh Bell.

Continued…

~ 2 ~

So you see we go to great lengths to ensure that all of our reindeer are adequately catered for, and I must confess that I am slightly surprised you are considering the possibility of an investigation. I can only conclude that somebody from the media has got hold of the story about the delay (which was totally unavoidable, as I explained at the time) in repairing the colour television in the Reindeer TV Lounge. Perhaps rumours about facilities being inadequate started that way.

These rumours are unfounded, as I hope you now realise, and if you would like to pay us a visit, you would be more than welcome. For instance, you could have a guided tour of the Reindeer Sleeping Quarters, where I think you will be most impressed with the standards of hygiene and tidiness.

A few of our reindeer occasionally let the organisation of their own cubicle fall below the standards expected [*Tinsel, check that Donner has emptied that Horlicks mug next to his bed; it's been there two days. Don't print this.*] but on the whole we find that individuals take great pride and pleasure in decorating the walls of their cubicles in interesting and appropriate ways. [*Also, tell Dancer her poster of James Bond will have to go. She's been warned already; it's her own fault. Remove it when she's not looking if you have to, but I want it off that wall today.*]

Continued…

~ 3 ~

I look forward to hearing from you soon, and perhaps I will also have the pleasure of welcoming you to my office, where I'm sure that Tinsel will be only too delighted to make us a jug of iced tea and we can chat about my commitment to maintaining a cruelty-free zone over a couple of Penguin biscuits.

Yours sincerely

Father Christmas

Tinsel, I have just been into my office. Get that James Bond poster off my wall immediately. Don't print this. And find something to occupy my mother or you'll be out on your wing.

12 March

Dear Mr Dinkela Esq

Thank you for your recent application for employment here at the North Pole. I am afraid, however, that having a vaguely Christmassy-sounding name and possessing a green pixie cap with a bell on it is not enough to secure you a post here in my grotto. Spraying your application with artificial snow and having it delivered by courier robin didn't help either. You mention nothing of your specialist qualifications: rosy cheeks, cheery whistle, rhythmical hammer-tapping skills, and so on. I'm afraid we do have a corporate image to maintain and we can't just take anyone who rolls up; I'd be up to my furry collar in highly ambitious baubles if that were the case.

Yours sincerely

Father Christmas

PS We'll return your robin once it's defrosted.

Well done, Tinsel. You may be a fairy of embarrassingly limited intellect, but you've certainly stumbled upon a brainwave this time. Letting Mother loose in the Dolls' House Annexe has kept her busy for hours. She keeps sending down requests for miniature dusters and scrubbing brushes, it's true, but I've assigned a dozen elves to keep her supplied with cleaning materials, and I've got my office to myself again! Tinsel, I owe you a huge debt of gratitude after this. How would you like to have the words 'FC's Personal Coffee-Bringer' added to your job description, as a boost for your career status? I'm nothing if not generous.

12 March

Dear Spencer Bradley-Morgan

Thank you for your exciting letter and invitation to join your club, The UFO Society. I am flattered that you saw fit to write to me and ask me to contribute descriptions of my own sightings to be included in your society's newsletter.

Over the years I have seen a number of curious objects in my travels, many of which I am unable to account for in any rational way, and I would be delighted to share my accounts of some of the most memorable.

It was a still, frosty night when the first of these experiences took place. I was flying high above the rooftops. (Rudolph had made some hot punch before we set off, and the reindeer were a bit friskier than usual).

Anyway, I suddenly became aware of a buzzing sound somewhere overhead. I looked up and saw it came from a moving object which had lights all along its length. I can't tell you the precise location of this sighting, I'm afraid; all I know is that it occurred very near to a local airport.

Even more mysterious was an object I saw on a different occasion, this time when I had parked on somebody's roof. Just as I was about to leave the sleigh I looked down over the side of the house and travelling quite close to the ground was a huge object with two different layers to it, both illuminated.

Now I know that people are always sceptical about UFOs, but I can swear to you that I actually saw beings of some description leave this object, and others enter it. I even thought I heard a fragment of primitive speech, which sounded like the phrase 'Tickets, please!' I defy anyone to explain *that* away scientifically.

Continued…

~ 2~

If you would like me to come down and give a talk about my experiences to your society, then do get in touch with me again. I'm sure that my input can only increase the respect and esteem with which the general public views you.

Yours sincerely

Father Christmas

PS It's not only at night that these inexplicable sightings occur, you know. For the last few days I've been seeing brightly-coloured, egg-shaped objects everywhere I look. And small beings with long floppy ears keep hopping out of cupboards. It's all most perplexing to a down-to-earth, sensible immortal such as myself.

Tinsel, I can't think why you're in such a temper. All I did was generously offer you a new privilege; most fairies would be grateful. Anyway, being sulky doesn't suit you; it makes your wings go all crumpled.

13 March

Dear Mr Bond

Thank you for your letter, one corner of which, unfortunately, seemed to be rather sticky. My Mother, a strict teetotaller, said it smelt to her of Martini; she looked quite shaken. I told her not to stir up trouble.

With regard to your presents: the 'wet suit' should be no problem; Mother is putting a dry suit into the washing machine even as we speak. Having said that, she is not at all happy with the idea of you wearing it wet, she says it's like giving you a Licence to Chill.

I'm afraid that your other request, the gadget-laden vehicle, has proven impossible to procure. Unfortunately, we at the North Pole have little access to cars of any sort, and as the penguins unanimously refused to part with their toboggans, I regret I cannot help you. [*Tinsel, this gives me an idea. Perhaps we might be able to claim for a few minor alterations to the sleigh as unavoidable expenses – a radar system, machine gun turret, ejector seat, that sort of thing? Nothing ostentatious, of course – there's nothing more pitiful than a middle-aged man trying to prop up his flagging masculinity with a lot of flashy, superficial gadgets.*]

Since we couldn't help you with the vehicle, I thought that as a goodwill gesture we should provide you with a romantic dinner with the kind of attractive female you are normally associated with, but this too is proving a bit tricky. Mother calculated that she would run out of clean corsets and support stockings if she attempted the trip to your hotel room, so that was out. Tinsel, too,

Continued…

~ 2 ~

when I broached the idea, looked less than pleased. In fact her face turned purple and her wand went into flame-thrower mode; I was lucky to escape with singed eyebrows and a blackened jacket. If any other ideas occur to me I will let you know, but I think it highly unlikely.

I remain, sir,

Your faithful servant

Christmas – Father Christmas

Tinsel, have you seen Dancer anywhere? I finally plucked up the courage to introduce her to Mother, but when we went to her cubicle her bikini and sun glasses had gone, and The Spy Who Loved Me *was blaring away on her CD player. Any idea where she may have got to?*

Tinsel, now that Mother's gone home, I've decided to reduce your workload by taking on another secretary, so please place the following advertisement in The Icicle *to see what kind of response we get. If that doesn't work we'll have to try* The Daily Snow.

WANTED - Polite and efficient fairy to work as a secretary for a busy organisation. Must have good telephone manner and be able to work harmoniously with others. Typing should be fast and accurate. The successful applicant will be required to travel between different offices, so flying licence must be clean (i.e. no grubby finger marks or coffee stains) and air tax and MOT up to date. Applicant must have own wings, which must be in good state of repair and full working order. Letters of application should be addressed to:
F. Christmas, c/o North Pole.
Closing date: 23rd March.

Tinsel, this is the only letter of application I received in response to the advert. See what you think?

Tasteful Sun-Lounger № 3
Deck of Private Yacht "The Albatross"
Somewhere in the Mediterranean

Father Christmas
Managing Director
The Grotto
North Pole

21 March

Dear Father Christmas

I am writing to reply to your charmingly idiosyncratic advertisement that appeared in this week's copy of The Icicle. I believe that I would be excellent at fulfilling the role in question, as I am a very efficient and organised fairy, with word-processing skills second to none and the unblemished flying licence that your require. I am able to 'work harmoniously with others' as long as those others are polite, well-bred fairies like myself, and not the sort of person who would play loud music on their personal stereo while in the office (I particularly dislike Bat Out of Hell) or make fun of my name. I have had previous experience as a secretary when I worked for a wonderful organisation whose aim was to promote the export of live animals across the continent. My hobbies are playing Monopoly and foxhunting.

I trust that you will give my application your fullest attention.

Yours sincerely

Angel Petherington-Withers

I think she sounds pompous, picky and snobbish. – Tinsel

My feelings exactly. We'll appoint her immediately – FC

April

1 April

Dear Goldilocks

Your suspicions about the 'foul old warders' at the detention centre were not justified, since I have received your letter safely, as you see. I fear I cannot arrange for your immediate release, even if you are bored with life behind bars; it also worries me that you do not appear to feel any kind of regret for the crimes that you've committed. Have you considered that the chair you broke may have had sentimental value, even if it didn't turn up trumps for you on *Flog It*? And sleeping in other people's beds may be acceptable in certain contexts: soap operas, reality TV shows, political circles etc, but it has clearly backfired on this occasion.

Breaking and entering is an offence, you know, and I have nothing but contempt for those unethical rascals who let themselves into properties while their owners are asleep, consume choice morsels of food at their expense, and then leave surreptitiously without taking any responsibility for the consequences of their nocturnal meddling.

I think if you do get parole you should be extremely careful as to how you conduct yourself in future. It may sound old-fashioned, but in my view little girls – and fairies, too for that matter – should be seen and not heard.

Yours disapprovingly

Father Christmas

Tinsel, Angel starts work in the office today. Try to take her under your wing a bit, will you? And by the way, arranging for the entire workforce to walk out just because I momentarily forgot the office rule forbidding spontaneous renditions of My Way *was a total over-reaction, even if it is April Fools Day. What's wrong with my singing anyway?*

8 April

Dear Mr Thompson

As someone who is particularly interested in the safety and welfare of all my employees – ranging from the most senior dwarf right down to the most junior fairy light – I am extremely glad that you contacted me regarding your concerns about our health and safety systems and procedures. I can assure you that all the correct documentation is in place, all the necessary equipment has been purchased, and all the practical arrangements have been made.

Our new Health and Safety Officer is Frankie, an elf who has recently been promoted from the packing department on account of her responsible attitude and the sterling work she has done there. Frankie has already proved herself to be a zealous and efficient worker. The number of fire extinguishers currently in the office now exceeds the required minimum by about 200 per cent. In fact, we have so many of the things we're tripping over them. There are also endless copies of the *Evacuation Procedures in Case of Fire* notices pinned upon every available wall and display board, as well as copies of the five hundred page *Causes of Fire: Potential Hazards* booklet, penned by Frankie herself, placed in a prominent position on every desk.

Continued…

~ 2 ~

This emphasis on following Health and Safety Regulations has been an inspiration to my whole staff. Even my secretary (who's not particularly quick-witted) was moved to comment that the office would be capable now of being transformed quite easily into a demonstration model for the emergency services to practise on. I seem to recall her exact words were: 'Somebody only needs to strike a match with all this paper around and we'll soon see what a *real* fire looks like ...' So we're definitely making progress.

Incidentally, in case you're concerned at my mention of striking matches in the office just now, let me reassure you that this is something that would never happen in any circumstances. Our non-smoking policy is strictly adhered to by all staff, even the inoffensive, solitary, victimised ex-pipe-smoker. I hope that the information I have given you in this letter resolves any doubts you may have entertained about the efficiency of our Health and Safety Procedures. If you would care to visit our office at any time, you would be more than welcome. Perhaps you'd like to drop in during one of our authentic, randomly timed fire drills, held at eleven o'clock prompt every Friday?

Yours, with policies and buckets of water for every occasion

Father Christmas

Tinsel, the question in my last memo was rhetorical. And anyway, some of the signatures on the petition were decidedly unconvincing. Since when have Christmas trees been able to write?

8 April

Dear Mr Alfonso

Your letter requesting clarification of my holiday booking arrived two weeks ago, but it turns out that my secretary has been using it as a drinks mat, hence the delay in replying. I simply wanted to reserve rooms at your hotel for myself and nine reindeer for the week beginning 7 August. I would like all the rooms to have balconies except for one (Dasher said he's had enough of high places, thank you) and it's essential that each has its own private bathroom. I know that my original booking was for eleven, but I neglected to check with my secretary beforehand; apparently she has made alternative plans and is going to spend her holiday backpacking around Thailand with a group of pixies.

In terms of the facilities, Comet is anxious that the table-tennis table will be in use this year. You remember that it was being mended last time we stayed at your hotel, and I'm afraid we had a few tears and tantrums as a result. He does take his table-tennis seriously. Also Rudolph particularly wants to try his hoof at wind-surfing, and I would like to confirm with you that an hour's tuition per day from a qualified instructor is included in the price of the holiday. Blitzen has asked me to check with you that the Hotel's Reading Room will be available for use by reindeer. He noticed the No Dogs sign last year, and is worried that this ruling may have been extended to apply to ruminants.

As I told you in my previous letter, we won't be flying (at least not with an airline company) and will make our own way to the hotel, where we look forward to meeting you at the Champagne Reception. The reindeer should enjoy it; they are pretty cosmopolitan in their tastes, although I have to say there were one or two raised eyebrows when I mentioned the finger buffet.

Continued...

~ 2 ~

I hope that this has answered your questions, and I look forward to exchanging my habitual winter garb for my short-sleeved shirt with fir-tree motif and matching bathing trunks in the near future.

Yours sincerely

Father Christmas

PS Cupid has requested that I remind you of your commitment to purchasing antler-proof basketballs following last year's unfortunate puncturing.

Tinsel, I've had a complaint from Angel about your behaviour. She says you keep being rude to her just because she works all through lunchtime and has already mastered the photocopier. Stop it instantly, Tinsel. That's an order.

9 April

Dear Molly

Thank you for your letter; what unusual lime-green writing paper! I'm afraid I wasn't able to appreciate it fully, as I have a severe headache, thanks to my secretary singing 'Wind Beneath my Wings' at the top of her voice for the last hour. She does it every time she's been on one of her inspection tours of local Hospitality and Beverage Centres, and it's really most inconsiderate. Especially as she always loops the loop when she gets to the chorus and puts her wand into 'glitter' mode; last time we were vacuuming fairy-dust out of filing cabinets for weeks.

Your request for two garden gnomes seems to me to be eminently reasonable, except that you've asked for the gnomes to be in specific poses – one holding a lantern, the other seated and holding a fishing rod. Although I'm sure the gnomes who volunteer for the job won't mind adopting these particular poses for some of the time, we can hardly expect them to stay like that indefinitely. I mean, it's not as if they're twelve inches tall and made of fibre-glass, is it?

Seriously, the gnomes in question would need to be given time off to eat, sleep and exercise, and they'd also need to be provided with proper changing and bathing facilities. It's not my place to put you under any pressure at all, but if you could see your way clear to making it possible for them to watch *Coronation Street*, I know how much they would appreciate it.

Continued…

~ 2 ~

Do let me know if you feel that you are unable to provide accommodation of a high enough standard. I have to warn you that without an environment that is suited to their needs gnomes do have a tendency to become unhappy. Many have even had to be rescued after flinging themselves into garden ponds. It is thought, though, that such desperation is only triggered by their inadvertently overhearing references to *Big Brother* or the *Eurovision Song Contest*, so as long as you bear that in mind all should be well.

Yours obligingly

Father Christmas

Tinsel, I didn't want you to stop the photocopier, you imbecile fairy. Ripping all the wires out like that has meant the machine will be out of action for the next week. Get the repairman in please. And try to exercise some common sense.

10 April

Dear Margaret

I was somewhat perplexed by your letter; it was written in such a polite, ladylike way that I felt I wanted to give you everything you asked for. However, getting your 'old job' back for you may not be possible, as the position has subsequently been filled by another person. I've had a word with him and he doesn't really want to relinquish the post, as he says it took him years of plotting to 'get this far'.

Casting my mind back over recent history, I would agree that talking politicians into hasty and ill-judged decisions is 'as easy as taking milk from a 5-year-old', but now that he's made his mind up, I'm not really sure what else I can do. Try waiting a while until he's ousted, perhaps?

Yours sincerely

Father Christmas

Tinsel, I've had a complaint from Angel about the way you've been carrying on with the repairman. She claims you keep fluttering your wings at him in a most unladylike manner. Try to have some consideration, Tinsel.

11 April

Dear Miss Scarlett

I received your letter yesterday but Tinsel, my secretary, filed it by mistake before I'd answered it. Too busy thinking about her new hairdo, or some other female nonsense, I dare say. You should have heard the fuss she made last week when she snagged one of her wings on the edge of the filing cabinet. She was so distressed she accidentally drop-kicked our smallest, most talkative goblin through a nearby window. Hardly the kind of rational, considered reaction we men are so famous for.

Speaking of men, I found the Christmas Trick that you want me to play on Dr Black, your employer, most intriguing. If I understand correctly, you want me to deliver an early Christmas present to Dr Black: some chocolates that you've had specially prepared by that helpful pharmacist friend you mention. You suggest I should leave them on the table in the library, being careful not to overturn the candlestick or trip over the lead piping.

I must also remember to drop a page from my diary in the room, so that Dr Black knows it's an authentic early Christmas gift. Also, if you happened to get any visitors – neighbours, relatives, forensic scientists – later on in the day, you'd be able to show them the diary page so that they could see his present was the 'genuine article'.

My congratulations, Miss Scarlett; you certainly know how to fool people. I suspect your employer will be completely speechless when he realises that you're

Continued…

~ 2 ~

the one who's secretly arranged all of this. I feel it's a particularly kind gesture for you to make, considering Dr Black's selfish behaviour this year. His writing off your Vintage Jaguar just before you got it insured must have been hard to forgive, and I don't know many employees who would allow their boss to play Barry Manilow music until 11 pm every night without exacting some kind of homicidal revenge.

All in all, I feel extremely privileged that you've asked me to be party to this amusing jape. I've even sent a copy of your letter to the local newspaper, I thought you should get full credit for your plan, and I look forward to seeing you hit the headlines in the very near future.

Yours appreciatively

Father Christmas

Tinsel, alright; 'unfairylike', not 'unladylike'. Angel says that the flowers the repairman sent you have brought on her allergy, so could you please move the vase(s) further away from her desk. She also says that the smell of your 'Rebel' perfume is exacerbating the problem. Stop being so selfish, Tinsel. The last thing we want in the office is a bad atmosphere.

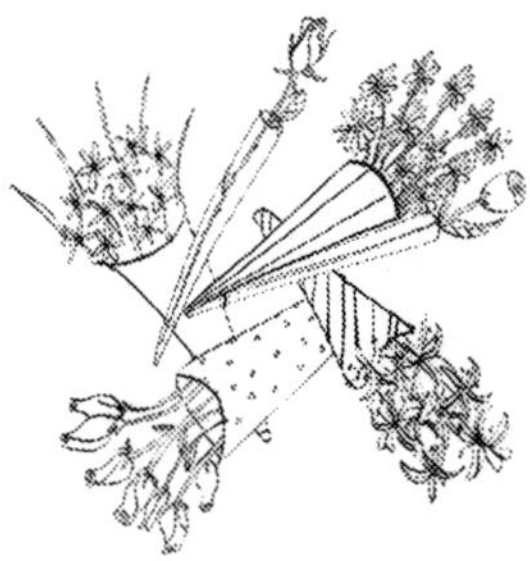

12 April

Dear Zak

Thank you for your letter and list of presents; I will see what I can do about the bird-eating spider, although I'm not making any promises. In response to your question: I believe I am covered by my insurance for injuries caused by livestock, although I really would have to check the small print.

It was good of you to enclose that map of your bedroom showing the whereabouts of your various pets so clearly; I shall be certain to keep very quiet when stepping over Rascal, your ferret, and Donna, your diamond-backed rattle snake, as you suggest.

It's so refreshing to hear from someone like yourself, who is genuinely concerned for the feelings of others. I couldn't believe it when I read that you wanted me to give Lindsay, your pet piranha, her Christmas lump of meat *by hand!* How many owners would be that considerate for the feelings of a mere fish? I'll certainly be delighted to oblige, and to extend the fingers of friendship to your aquatic little pal.

Yours, in eager anticipation

Father Christmas

Tinsel – Angel says that your new perfume, 'Outrage', is worse than the previous one, and is causing a bad atmosphere. She does not appreciate being called 'Fairy Poppins', and has said that she will hand in her notice if you carry on playing Bat Out of Hell *tapes on your personal stereo during office hours. She also wishes you to refrain from pinning 'Ban the Fur Trade' posters to the back of her white mink stole.*

Honestly, Tinsel, will you stop making things so difficult? You're only a secretary for goodness sake; it's not as if you're important. What's more, if Angel leaves, I'm holding you responsible.

---

13 April

Dear Red Riding Hood

I received your letter this morning; my secretary brought it in with my elevenses, and I have to tell you, Miss Hood, it caused me to choke on my slice of Battenburg. I couldn't believe that a young lady like you could possibly wish to acquire such unpleasant articles. Why do you want an anti-mugging spray, for goodness' sake? Or a set of wolf-sized pawcuffs? Some of the items on your list are simply too unpleasant for me to repeat, and I certainly will not be encouraging you in this ghastly tomboyish behaviour by putting them in your knee-length army sock as you request.

Instead, I've decided to present you with some gifts of my own choosing: a Barbie doll, some ballet shoes, and a toy vacuum cleaner. These are much more suitable, I feel, and much more useful than the unladylike objects you requested. How are you going to be able to keep your future husband's home spotlessly clean if you don't start practising your domestic skills now, while you're still young? That's the sort of thing with which you should be concerning yourself, not all this nonsense about self-defence. It's a question of priorities, Miss Hood.

Yours with deep concern

Father Christmas

Tinsel, Angel has just been to see me with a complaint that you are not pulling your weight in the office. Apparently, while she does all the filing and organises her desk-space for optimum efficiency, you merely sit there with your wings up reading a book entitled Business Take-over Bids and Personnel Management: An Advanced Guide. *This is not acceptable, Tinsel; you're skating on very thin ice. As senior secretary it's up to you to set a good example. Otherwise, if you're not careful, it will soon be Angel, not you, who's at the top of the tree.*

She's a fairy of many parts, after all.

21 April

Dear Charles

Your letter arrived this morning, and was nearly thrown away in error by Tinsel, my secretary (she's not very clever, I'm afraid). She showed it to me on her way to the recycling bin, saying, 'Here's more waste paper from another idiot.' However, I snatched it from her (I can be quite masterful, you know) and then demanded to judge for myself, while she went to get me a plaster from the first-aid box in the Reindeer locker-room. (She accidentally gave me quite a nasty scratch with one of her nails when I snatched the letter. I tend to forget how sensitive she is to any sort of sudden movement, the delicate little thing.)

So, now for your letter. Let me say first of all that I'm looking forward to visiting your house and seeing the huge collection of plants in your conservatory. I'm keen on plants myself, although I'm hopeless at remembering to water them. Tinsel loves plants and she's filled the office with ferns; the trouble is, they're always tumbling off the shelves onto my head. I sometimes say to her that she positions them deliberately so that that happens, and she always replies 'Absolutely'. It's nice to have a secretary with a sense of humour, I always think.

In terms of your requests, yes, of course I'll bring you the plant food and gardening books that you ask for. The concrete paving stones (340) might be a bit tricky, but I've told the reindeer to be positive and look on it as a challenge.

Continued…

~ 2 ~

I very much look forward to meeting all your wonderful plants and talking to them, as you tell me you do, hopefully at some length. I have a great respect and affection for our leafy brothers and sisters, and regret the fact that not everyone values them as much as plant-lovers like us.

Yours, with at least one green finger

Father Christmas

PS Do send my most grovelling respects to your mother.

Tinsel, one of your blasted ferns has just leapt off the shelf and hit me on the head again. I'm going to throw all of your stupid rotten plants in the bin if you can't train them to behave themselves better. Really, Tinsel.

22 April

Dear Mr Jarman

Your interesting letter arrived this morning, and I have to say I was intrigued by your proposals. Granting a request for ten large cans of spray-paint (three of them in luminous colours) should be easy; what I found most thrilling, though, was the invitation to join your 'On the Streets Artistic Workshop'. People often think my job is a glamorous one, and it is true that it does bring certain rewards – lots of free sherry, being able to visit a wide range of properties without being challenged … However, it's rare for me to have the opportunity in my line of work to express myself creatively, which is why the idea of participating in your 'hands-on' workshop is so exciting for me. I'll see you soon, and we shall certainly 'paint the town red' as they say (or in my case black and silver, with a flagrant flash of purple thrown in).

Here's to Art, Spray Cans and Life. Beauty is definitely on the wall of the householder.

Yours with nozzle poised

Father Christmas

Tinsel, I have here a five-page log Angel has kept of the occasions for complaint you have given her this morning so far. (I read it while I munched away at my elevenses, and it was so exhaustive that when I looked down a whole plate of brownies had gone.) This is totally unacceptable, Tinsel. I know she's new but she's flitted in very well. She always treats me with the utmost reverence and respect, and I don't want to lose her. You have a choice: extend the wing of friendship or leave. I'm sorry if that sounds stern, but we Christmases didn't get where we are today by being Mr Nice Guy. There's a pretty tough cookie lurking under this beard, I assure you. And sweep up those crumbs.

May

1 May

Dear Madam

I'm writing to query the telephone bill that I received this morning, as frankly, I consider the sum demanded to be exorbitant. The bill you have sent me is nearly twice what it was last quarter, and I'm completely unable to account for the sudden increase. I haven't been using the phone any more than usual, and am certain that none of my staff has.

My secretary, Tinsel, is friendly with a rather undesirable elf called Ringo Redjacket, who now lives in New York, and even though in general he is completely unsympathetic to any of my problems, Tinsel told me that even he said our phone bill was 'a bit steep'. They discussed it at some length, apparently.

I would ask that you reduce our bill to its normal amount; otherwise I will be forced to examine other possible methods of communicating with the outside world.

Yours, becoming quite hot under the (furry) collar

Father Christmas

Tinsel, how are those penguins coming on with their flying lessons?

* * *

Memo
To: *Tinsel*
From: *Father Christmas*
Re: *Angel's resignation*
Tinsel, I thought you might care to see the attached letter, which arrived from Angel's mother this morning:

Blue Horizon Bluff
St. Margaret's Road
Oxford
England

3 May

Dear Mr Christmas

I regret to inform you that my daughter, Angel Petherington-Withers, has decided that she no longer wishes to work for your organisation. She has asked me to notify you in writing of this decision (which takes effect immediately) as she fell victim to one of her migraines after flying home, so I've packed her off to bed with her favourite stuffed pony.

Ever since Angel's arrival in your office, your personal secretary (I believe her name is Tinsel) has gone out of her way to make things difficult for my daughter. She has persisted in distracting Angel from her work by playing loud and unpleasant so-called music on her personal stereo, right next to Angel's workspace. When Angel wrote a polite note to Tinsel asking her to stop listening to this racket during office hours, Tinsel's response was to tear the note into tiny pieces, put them in a plastic cup, and rattle it in time to the music.

Now, Mr Christmas, it's not for me to tell you how to run your own business, but I do think you should consider dismissing this Tinsel-creature, as she clearly has no respect whatsoever for traditional values. Angel tells me she is not even in favour of foxhunting - need I say more?

Yours sincerely

Cynthia Petherington-Withers

So, Tinsel ... I'll see you in my office straight after the Bank Holiday weekend. I would prefer to deal with you immediately, but unfortunately I can't, as I have to read my other letters. There's one here, I see, from a Flight Lieutenant. That's the sort of person who writes to me, Tinsel. Men of rank and action. In their eyes I'm a worthy public figure – not an employer whose word can be flouted, as certain red-headed fairies seem to think. Your days in this office are definitely numbered. (Not that you'd be intelligent enough to count them, lowly and brainless typist that you are.)

---

3 May

Dear Flight-Lieutenant Calgar

Thank you so much for your kind invitation to join you and your fellow 'Red Arrows' for a special Christmas flying display next year. The idea of looping the loop in my sleigh almost turns my stomach to jelly, it's so exciting.

Unfortunately, however, I have to decline this tempting offer. I would like to point out that this is not because of any cowardice on my part. Nothing would please me more than to have the wind whistling through my beard several hundred feet up in the air. It's just that I have to consider my staff. Although I myself feel quite exhilarated about the prospect of dicing with certain death, it is my obligation to protect the reindeer in my charge from taking any unnecessary risks. Also, the presents might fall out of the sleigh.

Continued…

~ 2 ~

Another reservation I have is that I am only used to making nocturnal flights, and I am concerned that I might find flying in daylight somewhat unnerving. Usually, you see, if I have a near-miss with an awkwardly placed chimney stack, I don't really know about it, but your aerobatics displays are brimming with near-misses, all of them orchestrated in Technicolor daylight. I feel that the shock of such experiences might be a little difficult for me to cope with, technically speaking.

I am also concerned that my relatives would become very anxious if they knew I was planning to participate in such a dangerous enterprise. My Great Aunt Belinda would be particularly worried about it, I know, and she's such a frail old thing, I'd really hate to cause her any sort of alarm.

All in all, then, I fear I must decline your invitation, tempting as it is. It's a great pity I won't get to meet you and your colleagues – why don't you fly down here instead? Then we could all get together anyway, for a bracing game of tiddlywinks, perhaps?

Yours sincerely

Father Christmas

Tinsel, forget about my rather hasty memo. I hope you had a pleasant Bank Holiday weekend? I have just received this terrifying message from my Great Aunt Belinda.

Christmas, my boy, what nonsense is this about you refusing to do a flying display with the Red Arrows? Tom Calgar said you had chickened out of it. No need to worry about the danger, you silly child; I go parachuting with the Red Arrows every week and it's perfectly safe. Must close now – am off on safari to Kenya. Sure you don't want to accompany me? Or how about that fiery little secretary of yours? Am sending her a ticket in case she'd enjoy the change of scene. Must fly. Pilot's here.

Will drop in on you soon.

Belinda

Return it. Ask her not to visit. Tell her I'm busy collecting mistletoe samples in an obscure South American rainforest. Anything! I'm sure I can rely on your loyalty after everything I've done for you?

5 May

Dear Sara^^Short^^^^

()

Think you for your litter; things are bgrather fraught here at the office right now because my secretary has disappeared, but I will try to bring you everyring you asked for. I've no idel where she's got too,, apparently she bought lots of suntan lotion and insect repellent and then hired a husky to take her to the airport. It's very worryingxx and most inconvenient as I can't find a new jam of coffee she bought for the office last week and I'm having to do all my own typing. It just isn't ike her to run off and leavee me like this; I'm sure my mad Great Aunt hades something to do with it. Anyway – your letter – yes, I'll"" bring you … what waszz it you wanted? Oh that's right, the Crown Jewels: I'll send some gnomes to London00 to pick them up for you in there moaning. Where could!! she have got to? That's what I want to now …

Yours sincerely***

___%%

Further Christmas

10 May

Dear Brodie

Your letter arrived from Australia last week, but my secretary is on holiday in Kenya at the moment, apparently, and everything here is rather chaotic as a result. A couple of her friends have taken over her work in the office while she's gone, but they are so strict with me, I'm almost afraid to go in there. One particularly bossy one – Sparkles, her name is – insisted I buy a proper coffee machine, so we are having filter coffee now. Which is all very well in its way, but guess who gets landed with making it?

In response to your question: no, I'm afraid you can't borrow my clothes to use as a costume for a fancy-dress party. You might tear them or drop wine on them or something, and my life is complicated enough as it is at the moment without having to worry about removing Beaujolais '98 stains from my furry collar.

Sorry to disappoint you, but I've got other things to think about right now. Why doesn't she even send me a postcard? She knows where I am …

Yours sincerely

Father Christmas

LATTE
SPARKLES
CHIEF SECRETARY

12 May

Dear Cinderella

Thank you for your letter; sorry about the watermarks but I couldn't find a cloth to dry my hands on after washing up all the coffee cups. In response to your request: could I 'wave a magic wand' and make it possible for you to 'go to the king's ball?' – no, I certainly couldn't. Girls your age are better off staying at home nights, revising for their exams, not gadding off to dances and parties, and places like Kenya on ridiculous flights of fancy, without telling anyone where they're going.

The prince is not going to fall in love with you at first sight and sweep you off your feet, you know. You're more likely to be bitten by mosquitoes, or crushed by a trunkful of marauding elephants (or whatever the collective noun for elephants is). It's a jungle out there and you'd be much better off staying at home.

If you decide to ignore this excellent advice, then you're a very silly young girl indeed. Promise me that if you do go to this 'ball' affair, you'll at least spray yourself with insect repellent first, and *wear sensible footwear.*

Yours, shaking his head in disapproval

Father Christmas

24 May

Dear Eve

Your letter arrived four days ago, and I haven't answered it before now because I couldn't be bothered. I've got more important things on my mind. Just one postcard! That's all I ask.

I suppose you think it's amusing, do you, making fun of a man because his secretary's left him? Requesting an untouched apple indeed, what a ridiculous present to ask for. Are you suggesting I'm too incompetent to procure anything better; that the whole operation here has fallen to pieces, simply because of the departure of one red-headed fairy? I'm managing perfectly well, thank you, and I can do without snide comments from the likes of you. If you want an apple, I suggest you find yourself an orchard and pick one.

Women! If only they knew how much suffering they cause …

Yours in deep disgust

Father Christmas

28 May

Dear Kitty

I received your letter some time ago but have been too busy running around after a couple of idle fairies, who want organic, Fairtrade filter coffee on demand, to get the chance to answer it. Thank you for your modest list of presents; yes, I will certainly send you the fountain pen and writing paper that you require. I suppose that, as an agony aunt, you must get through forestfuls of the stuff, writing to all those people who are going through a difficult time in their lives. People who've lost their job, for instance, or whose fairy lights are worrying them, or whose secretary has just gone off on a safari without so much as a by your leave, and hasn't even bothered sending a postcard home.

I've got a friend in that situation actually, a very nice chap, his secretary simply walked out suddenly one day to go to Kenya, and he's feeling exceedingly put out about it. Apparently she hasn't even sent him a postcard; I believe his feelings are quite sore on the subject. He can just about cope in the office, with the help of her two friends, but things don't seem the same without her there. He misses the way she used to accidentally staple his beard to his desk, and spill coffee over all his vital paperwork. His correspondence now looks sort of bare, as if something is missing, without those familiar splashes.

He doesn't even know how long she's going to be gone for – this could be just the tip of the iceberg. What should I advise my friend to do, do you think? He dreamed last night she was being swallowed by a fairy-eating, sugar-frosted Yule log.

Continued…

~ 2 ~

She's such a helpless little thing; anything could happen out there. Danger surrounds all of us every minute, and can strike at any time, so how can anyone feel safe? To take a ridiculously improbable example: now, at this very moment, a heavy object could come hurtling through the roof above my head and knock me out –

* * *

Sorry about the two-week gap between this and the last entry, it's just that a heavy object came hurtling through the roof above my head and knocked me out. It was my secretary, parachuting out of a plane piloted by my Great Aunt. She just had time to thank me for breaking her fall, and to explain that the line between ridiculous improbability and narrative inevitability is a fine one, before I passed out.

I've been in hospital ever since, and this is the first day the nurses have allowed me to have my pad and pen. I'm not very keen on these nurses; they're extremely bossy. If it wasn't for Blitzen smuggling in bottles of Babycham left over from the Reindeer Christmas Party, I don't know what I'd do. I can't wait to get out of here, but apparently I've got to stay until my concussion gets better. Ridiculous! I'm not concussed … That's what I told those anxious musical cuttlefish, and that's what I'm telling you. I don't have the faintest idea why I'm writing to you, by the way, and in any case, I've got to close now as some ballet-dancing cushions have arrived and they want me to audition for a leading role in *Swan Lake*. Apparently I'm up against some prominent Liberal Democrats, so it's going to be very tough.

Yours in some confusion

Father Christmas

14 June

Dear Albert

Thank you for your Get Well card; it's always good to hear from my favourite nephew. In response to your kind enquiries: no, I'm not doing too badly, and yes, I should make it to the end of the week. I find it very touching that you're concerned with my legal as well as physical welfare at a time like this, but in answer to your questions, yes, I have made out a will, and no, I'm not going to do what some of these 'daft old fogies' do and donate all my money to a local Cats' Refuge. I should think not. No, all of my money is going to a charity close to my heart: The Reginald Reindeer Memorial Home for Retired Mincepies. And now I can feel my concussion coming on again, so I'd better close before the laundry baskets find out I've been writing to you.

See you soon, I expect,

Your loving uncle

xxxxxx

[Pet name as before. Tinsel, should we take pity on him since he's in hospital? – Ed.]

Maybe. There's always the chance of a sequel. – Tinsel

16 June

Dear Spike

Thank you for your letter, which the hospital postman delivered to me this morning. That is to say, he flung it in the direction of my pillow, slicing the heads off the white carnations that Blitzen had brought me. I'd probably be minus a beard if I hadn't ducked.

Anyway, back to your letter. It was so friendly and sympathetic; you really seemed to understand how I feel, being cooped up in this place. You say your own accommodation is fairly similar: one small cell, no freedom to come and go as you please, limited visiting hours, grim-faced staff, who wake you at unearthly hours for the sheer fun of it. Are you sure you're not in the next ward?

I must say, your request for a present was extremely modest – all you want for Christmas, so you tell me, is 'the key'. 'Key to what?' I wondered initially, but since you didn't specify, I assumed that it didn't matter, so I'm sending you the key to one of the broken lockers in the Reindeer Changing Rooms. I hope that's alright.

I'm afraid I have got to go now, as Blitzen's just arrived, and has discovered from one of the nurses the identity of the careless carnation decapitator, so he's started beating the hospital postman about the head with a rolled-up newspaper, pausing occasionally to pelt him with Glacier Mints. A world in which a mild-mannered ruminant becomes enraged over a slightly indifferent flower arrangement is a very strange one.

Yours in some bemusement

Father Christmas

Press Release

To: Editor of *The Icicle*
From: Father Christmas
Date: 18 June
Re: Photo opportunity

You may be interested to know that I have recovered from my recent indisposition and will be leaving hospital tomorrow at 10.00 am (so that the bed can be prepared for the next patient, arriving at 10.03 am). Your journalists may want to photograph this important occasion, and I have also prepared a statement to the press, which they may wish to record (estimated running time: 3 hours 40 minutes, refreshments will be provided during the interval). I expect you will want to devote your front page and several articles to this story, or perhaps it could be turned into a serial, running for a number of weeks.

Speaking of serials, my breakfast has just arrived, so I'd better start retrieving Ice Krispies from the furthest reaches of my pillow case.

No doubt I'll see you tomorrow.

Father Christmas

19 June

Dear Laurel

I received your letter yesterday – the first that's arrived since I was released from hospital – but frankly, I've been too upset to answer it until now; events have taken such a dramatic and hideous turn. I was incarcerated in that awful place for over a week, and at the end of my stay I sent a press release to the editor of the local paper, so that he could have a fleet of journalists waiting for me as I left. And what happens? One spotty youth shows up and announces that he's on a Youth Training Scheme and has come as the newspaper's sole representative. I was furious! Being forced to deliver my statement to an audience of one; it was humiliating.

More people were there for some of the time, it's true, but they didn't seem to be giving me their full attention – instead they kept gathering round these large white vans carrying lazy individuals on mobile beds. Some of them were quite rude, actually; they shouted things like 'Don't block the Emergency Entrance, you stupid idiot', and brandished bits of medical equipment in the air, quite aggressively, I thought. Anyway, I told the Youth Training Scheme lad not to worry about them calling him a stupid idiot – he'd have to get used to worse names than that if he went into journalism – and carried on with my speech. He clapped bravely at the end, but it wasn't what I'd envisaged, not the cheering, applauding mob I'd set my heart on …

Continued…

~ 2 ~

Anyway, just when I thought that things couldn't get any worse, I asked the Youth Training Scheme lad where the rest of the staff from his paper were. After all, I thought, it may be that some amazing story had broken elsewhere – perhaps some vicious, unprincipled editor had got hold of the private memos of a renowned public figure and published them, something like that. But no, it transpired they'd all gone to cover a story about an office, where a secretary had taken charge in her boss's absence and had revolutionised the whole organisation: pay scales, job descriptions, the works. Poor man, I thought, imagine going back to that after you've been away – what a nightmare.

So I said goodbye to the Youth Training Scheme lad and waited for Blitzen to arrive to take me back to my nice, familiar workshop. I thought he was rather subdued, but didn't understand why until we arrived and I saw the hordes of press and TV people … I'm sorry. I can't write any more. You'll just have to forget your gift, whatever it was. Some moments are simply too painful for me to dwell upon.

Yours in abject misery

Father Christmas

Tinsel – could I please make an appointment to see you as soon as it's convenient? Sparkles said I'd have to ask when there was a space in your diary. Perhaps straight after your mid-morning coffee and cream cakes tomorrow?

I've checked with the reindeer and they say that they should be able to spare me. I've made up the time I spent writing to the last correspondent. I'm sorry about that lapse, but old habits die hard, and I haven't adjusted properly yet to fulfilling my new job description.

I must confess that when you outlined my new role, and said you wanted me to be 'in harness' more, I did assume you were speaking metaphorically. However, I realise that taking my turn at the less glamorous aspects of gift-delivery is, as you point out, much fairer, especially since the group I work with has been re-trained and re-named the 'Sleigh-Pulling Reindeer Collective'. I accept that Rudolph's promotion meant there was a need for Ruminant Role Re-structuring, and am sure that in time the (pale pink) wings you have lent me will enable me to 'pull my weight' more effectively when airborne.

It's just that I wanted to ask you about a rumour that you are planning to sabotage the book I was writing by mixing some of my private correspondence in with those letters I want included just before they are sent off to the publisher. I want to make it quite clear, Tinsel – I mean, I'd like to request – that you put all such thoughts completely out of your head. I am – was? – am a respected public figure, and I do not wish to become the laughing stock of the nation through the irresponsible behaviour of one fairy. I don't want to hear another word on the subject, Tinsel, and I don't care if you are in charge now; NONE of my private correspondence – including my memos to you – is to be sent to the publisher, and that is FINAL. Do you understand me, Tinsel? Final.

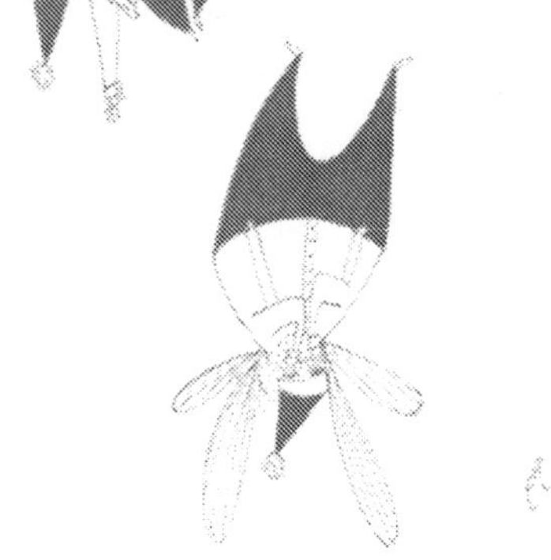

Editor's note:

After these letters went to press it was realised that some had inadvertently been included that were internal memos, or came from Father Christmas' private correspondence. Unfortunately it was too late to retrieve them, so I would like to offer my apologies to all concerned – Ed.

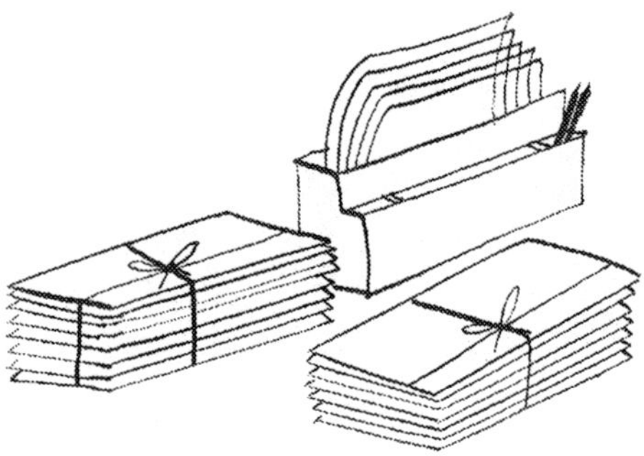

Afterword

1 July

Dear Reader

It has come to my attention that vicious rumours have been circulating to the effect that Father Christmas, in his traditional role, still, in fact, exists. Clearly this is a preposterous notion, and the book that you (continue to) hold in your hands is concrete (well, hard copy) proof against such ridiculous allegations. Were it not such a petty, unseasonable threat to make, I would feel tempted to suggest that anyone who claims still to believe in FC will be off my Christmas list faster than you can say 'Compulsory Redundancy Package'.

I would like, therefore, to take this opportunity to explain that FC's previous role has been abolished; he now goes by the title of Mr Claus and is part of the newly formed Sleigh-Pulling Reindeer Collective, housed in a cubicle similar to those of his ruminant colleagues.

The task of responding to requests for presents, sent in by the general public, has consequently fallen to myself as Managing Director, and I would like to assure my readers that the service now offered is far more efficient and likely to produce much higher levels of satisfaction than that 'managed' – I use the term in its loosest sense – by my predecessor.

Continued...

~2~

It only remains for me to wish you all a very merry Christmas,

Regards

Tinsel

Sparkles, I wouldn't mind a coffee if you've got a minute. Don't print this, obviously...

Breinigsville, PA USA
29 December 2010

252385BV00001B/22/A

9 781905 621972